"Subject, Timothy Parish;
autopsy 691-337-21," he began.

"Caucasian male. Age eighteen. Height, five feet eleven inches; weight, two hundred and twelve pounds. Visual examination reveals contusions, probably received when subject collapsed. Tattoo on left shoulder of Greek comedy and tragedy masks. Faded surgical scar on right knee. No other external markings. Rigor is severe, but an odd lack of settling of the blood is noted."

Jenna watched as Slick brought the scalpel up and placed its tip where he always did, at the center of the chest, over the breastbone. Her mind went back to the party two nights earlier, and her efforts to save the frat boy.

She was glad to be back on the job. Jenna knew she had made the right decision.

Slick pressed the tip of the scalpel down, and the skin dimpled for a moment, then split. The M.E. dragged the blade carefully down the center of the dead kid's chest. Three inches. Four.

There was blood.

Then Tim Parish opened his eyes wide, and began to scream.

Body of Evidence thrillers
by Christopher Golden

Body Bags
Thief of Hearts
Soul Survivor
Meets the Eye
Head Games

christopher golden
MEETS the EYE

A *Body of Evidence* thriller starring Jenna Blake

SIMON PULSE
New York London Toronto Sydney Singapore

First Simon Pulse edition December 2002
First Pocket Pulse edition February 2000
Text copyright © 2000 by Christopher Golden

SIMON PULSE
An imprint of Simon & Schuster
Children's Publishing Division
1230 Avenue of the Americas
New York, NY 10020

Printed in USA

10 9 8 7 6 5 4 3

ISBN 0-671-03495-2

for Jean-marc Joseph

acknowledgments

Thanks, as always, to my editor, Lisa Clancy, and everyone at Pocket, as well as my agent, Lori Perkins. Thanks to Dr. Brian M. Golden for arcane medical texts, and to Dr. Jennifer Keates for her expertise on burial customs. Finally, as always, thanks to my sons, Nicholas and Daniel, who are the light of my life, and especially to Connie, my wife and partner.

MEETS the EYE

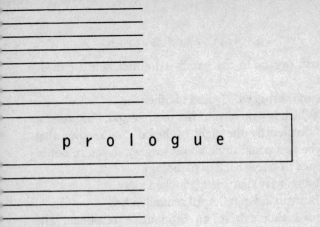

The dead don't scare me," Jenna Blake said. "That's not what it's about."

On the other side of the dining room table, which was laden with a lavish Thanksgiving Day meal, her mother looked dubious. Before April Blake could question her daughter's words, Jenna went on.

"It's true," she said. "I don't get any of those creepy feelings in the autopsy room. Even being at the scene of a murder or an accident doesn't really bother me. Sure, it's nasty, and it's sad—on a scale of one to yuck it's up there. But none of that bothers me."

Jenna glanced at Yoshiko Kitsuta, her roommate at Somerset University, whom she'd brought home to share Thanksgiving at the Blakes', since it would have been too expensive for Yoshiko to fly home to Hawaii just for the weekend.

Yoshiko smiled. "Which is what makes you weird," she told Jenna. "If somebody wanted me to hold fresh human organs in my hands, I'd either faint or throw up."

Jenna shrugged. "Doesn't bother me."

"Which is wonderful," her mother said. "You used to be horrified by the sight of blood. You're over that. Maybe you could think about surgery, if you're not interested in going back to pathology."

"I didn't say that." Jenna looked away.

"But you *did* quit," April reminded her.

Jenna didn't have an immediate response. Her mother was right. She'd been working as a diener, or pathology assistant, at Somerset Medical Center, and loving every minute of it. Puzzles had always intrigued her, and she was enthralled by the idea of solving the puzzles that each autopsy presented, while bringing peace of mind to the relatives of the deceased. But she had a tendency toward the forensic end of pathology, toward figuring out not only what had happened, but why and how. Several times, it had put her in harm's way.

"It wasn't just that I was afraid," Jenna said, glancing away. "It wasn't just the danger."

April offered a slight shrug. "Well, you won't get any argument from me, honey. I'm just relieved you're out of there. If Dr. Slikowski were your average medical examiner, I wouldn't worry so much. But he gets too involved in these cases. It isn't safe." She stood up and smiled at the two girls. "So, who's for apple pie à la mode?"

Both Jenna and Yoshiko agreed that pie was very necessary. After April had gone into the kitchen, though, Yoshiko looked at Jenna with concern.

"You're waffling," Yoshiko observed. "It's spooking her. You said you weren't going back."

"I'm not," Jenna said, but even she didn't think it sounded convincing. So she said it more firmly. "I'm *not.*"

That's a little better, she thought.

Yoshiko studied her a moment. "So, if it doesn't bother you hanging around dead people, and the danger isn't enough to scare you off, what is it?"

Jenna took a long breath and let it out, contemplating Yoshiko's question. It was the very thing she'd been grappling with in the weeks since she'd quit her job. Even on the drive home to Natick the previous night, her mind hadn't been on the road, or Thanksgiving, or the perfect fall evening, with the smell of wood burning in fireplaces that permeated the air when she got out of the car in front of her mother's house. She and Yoshiko didn't even talk that much on the drive out, though she'd been a little better today.

Can you say "preoccupied"?

Jenna smiled and looked at Yoshiko, who was waiting for an answer.

"I guess it's the insanity," she said at length. "The twisted, sick minds of the people who do this stuff. Maybe they're nuts or maybe they're evil or maybe they're just born without whatever it is that makes the rest of us human, but it makes me sick, Yosh. It's not even that it terrifies me as much as it makes me feel filthy, like I should be ashamed that I'm part of the same species that can turn out monsters like that.

"I just got tired of feeling that way," Jenna said sadly.

"Wow," Yoshiko said softly. "I don't blame you. On

the other hand, I've got to say, you still don't sound one hundred percent, y'know?"

Jenna thought about it, her mind straying from the danger and the horror to the good she'd done as part of Slick's team. Their work had helped to stop at least two killers. She might even have saved lives by working to solve those mysteries. She . . .

No.

"I'm not going back," Jenna said firmly.

Jason Castillo had been working Boston P.D.'s narcotics division for seven years. In that time, he'd sat waiting for a drug deal to go down almost more often than he'd sat at his dinner table to eat. He was thirty-three, divorced, no children. His life was the job. The job was fishing.

That's how Castillo looked at it, anyway. Cast out the line, hook a little fish, maybe give it some play, let it run until it became bait for the big one, the real score. Right up the food chain. In that seven years, he'd seen all kinds of ways it could go down. Maybe the buy wouldn't happen, the deal would be off. Maybe it'd go down smoothly and they'd send a couple of scumbags to jail. Two years ago, Castillo had his biggest bust, more than a thousand pounds of heroin on a boat in Boston Harbor. He'd made the news for that one.

Yeah, it was nice when it all went according to plan.

Sometimes, though, all hell would break loose, and things would get very, very messy.

But in seven years, Jason Castillo had never seen anything like this.

In an alley across the street, a bunch of gangbangers calling themselves the Dorchester Kings were about to hand over a bag full of cash for a suitcase loaded with enough swag to net a quarter of a million dollars on the street. It was the heroin deal they thought would put them in the big time. But the Kings didn't know they had a mole. Boston P.D. had a man inside, wired for sound.

Greg Tarver was new to the narcotics division, but this bust was going to give him a solid start, no doubt. To nail not just the Kings, but the courier who brought the swag and made the switch. The idea was to get the courier to give up his boss, Antonio Micellatti. Micellatti ran an import-and-export business, but it was pretty clear to the cops that he specialized in the import end of things.

So that was the setup. Castillo sat in a coffee shop across the street from the alley with a wire trailing up to the receiver in his ear. The other cops in his unit were spread out, ready to take the entire deal apart. Three of them were in a van half a block away, listening very carefully to what was going down. Two more in a nearby car, pretending to have a lovers' quarrel. Detective Sergeant Pete Karasiotis was digging through garbage bins for returnable cans and bottles. And Castillo sipped his coffee and watched the Dorchester Kings roll on up in their rumbling, barely street-legal rides.

They spilled out of the two cars, leaving the drivers

behind, ready to go. Five guys went into the alley, glancing around, looking for trouble. Castillo sipped his coffee and waited right along with them. None of them had long to wait. Three minutes after the Kings entered the alley, the courier appeared, walking at a steady clip along the sidewalk, a heavy suitcase in his hand.

"Christ, these guys are fearless," Castillo muttered to himself. *That's what they think of our legal system,* he thought. *Take a bust, and my lawyer has me out in time for breakfast.*

"Not this time," he whispered over the rim of his coffee cup.

In his ear, he could hear the conversation begin, thanks to Tarver's wire. The bluster, the bullshit male posturing. The Kings tested the merchandise, and then the courier zipped his suitcase again. They started to make the trade.

Castillo grabbed the walkie-talkie clipped to his belt. "Do it," he barked.

But even as he headed for the door, something went terribly wrong. He heard shouting, threats. Someone had come into the alley who wasn't supposed to be there. Castillo's first thought was that it was a civilian, stumbling into the wrong place at the wrong time. A civilian who was about to die.

Then the gunfire started.

With a curse, he pushed out the door of the coffee shop, unclipped his service weapon from its holster, and bolted across the street toward the alley. Pete Karasiotis met him halfway.

"What the hell—" Castillo started.

"Someone else showed up. Solo!" Karasiotis blurted in astonishment. "Guy just went in and opened fire!"

Castillo thought the other cop had more to say, but then a bullet punched through Karasiotis's skull at the temple, and the man went down in a bloody sprawl on the street.

There wasn't time for Castillo to report in. It didn't matter anyway. He knew the others would be coming in. Even now, the rest of the unit was moving on his position. It would be only seconds before they arrived.

Castillo didn't have seconds.

At the mouth of the alley stood a man dressed in a rumpled, blood-spattered suit. He had the suitcase full of swag and the bag of cash clutched in his right hand, and a gun in the other. Apparently one dead cop wasn't enough for him, because he opened fire even as Castillo aimed his own weapon.

The hollow pop of gunfire thudded dully from the blind faces of gray buildings. A bullet tore through Castillo's shoulder, hard enough to spin him sideways. In shock, wound burning, bleeding, he went down. He tried to lift his weapon, to take aim, but the guy was above him then.

The shooter's face was white and pale and expressionless, like he was bored, or about to fall asleep. His eyes barely registered Castillo, or anything else for that matter. He looked almost dead as he pointed the gun at Castillo's forehead.

Gunfire ripped through the night again, and the shooter jittered, dropping what he'd stolen as bullets punctured his chest and abdomen and leg. He crumpled to the ground next to Castillo, and the cop sat up, one hand on his wound and the other holding his weapon steady, waiting to see if the guy would rise.

The shooter never got up. He bled out, there on the street, not far from the load of money and heroin he'd killed for, and died for. Castillo gritted his teeth with the pain in his shoulder and stared in mute fury at the dead man.

"Ain't this a fiasco?" muttered Ned Schulman as he came up behind Castillo. "Ambulance is on the way, Jace. The skels driving for the Kings took off as soon as the shooting started. What the hell happened?"

Castillo shook his head, trying to make sense of it. The shooter must have been working solo, but nobody was that crazy. Even if you knew the deal was going down, even if you could kill a bunch of gangbangers and drug dealers and walk away with the profits, no way would it go unavenged. The guy had to have been nuts.

He looked nuts, that was for sure. *Or something.* Castillo was stumped. Two good cops were dead, probably all of his suspects too, and he had no idea why.

"God, Jace, did you take a look at this guy?" Schulman asked, shocked.

Castillo frowned, having a hard time focusing on anything but the wound in his shoulder and the sound of the siren from the approaching ambulance. But he managed to turn and look at the shooter's face.

"You know him?" Castillo asked.

"*You* know him," Schulman insisted. "It's that reporter. Cohen."

"What? From the *Globe?*"

"That's him."

Incredulous, Castillo took a closer look. He hadn't seen Marc Cohen in person in a couple of years, but it looked like Schulman was right.

Which was impossible.

"Can't be," Castillo said. "Cohen's been dead almost a month. Heart attack."

"Yeah? Tell me who this is, then."

But Jason Castillo didn't have an answer for that.

c h a p t e r   1

Finals were still a few weeks away, but Jenna didn't think it was too soon to start completely freaking out. It was just after three o'clock, the Sunday after Thanksgiving, and she was back at Somerset, in her room at Sparrow Hall. Though it was cold outside, she was pretty sure she could have come up with something better to do than study. She was in the middle of reading *Comanche Moon*, by Larry McMurtry, and had just discovered a wonderfully eccentric series of mystery novels by Don Winslow. She had lots of fun, recreational reading she could have been doing.

Instead, bio.

With a deep sigh, Jenna tore her gaze away from the cold blue sky and the swaying, skeletal branches of the leafless trees outside the window. One of her guilty pleasures—pre-self-discovery Madonna—grooved quietly on the CD player. It wasn't something she played loud. On the other hand, Amie-down-the-hall seemed content to blast Backstreet Boys, so Jenna didn't know why she bothered being ashamed.

She read several more pages in her biology text, finishing up a chapter she'd read twice earlier in the semester. Then she picked up her notebook and flipped to the pages from the corresponding class discussion. With relief, she realized that she'd taken better notes than she'd remembered. If she studied those, she thought she might not have to go back to the textbook after all.

"Very cool," she said softly, nodding.

With that small triumph, though she knew biology really required more time, she decided to move on to her European history notes. She wanted to familiarize herself with the big picture, as far as what they'd covered in class, so she could draw parallels between various events for the essay part of the final.

Jenna had never been quite so conscientious about such things, but she'd missed a number of classes this semester and didn't want to suffer for it.

She'd been leaning against a stack of pillows that were bunched up against her bed—she had the lower bunk, while Yoshiko had the top—but now she got up and stretched.

Just a little break, she told herself. *Studying requires chocolate.*

Oreos weren't exactly what she wanted, but they'd do. She went over to the cabinet where she and Yoshiko kept what little food they had in the room. Just as she reached in for the half-empty bag of cookies, there was a knock on the door.

Jenna glanced questioningly at the door, then back at the Oreos.

"Don't go away," she told the cookies.

She opened the door to find Hunter LaChance standing in the hallway, looking rumpled and tired. He hadn't really wanted to spend Thanksgiving weekend with his mother in Louisiana, but had felt obligated to go. Hunter's sister, Melody, who had been Jenna's best friend, had been murdered earlier in the semester, and his father had died years before. Hunter was all his mother had left.

"Hey!" Jenna said, genuinely happy to see him. And not just because it meant a break from studying.

With a grin, she gave Hunter a squeeze, and then let him into the room. "Yoshiko's at the library," she told him. "But she'll be back soon. How was your flight?"

"It was okay," Hunter replied noncommittally. "Did you-all have a nice Thanksgiving?"

"Yeah," Jenna agreed. "My mom made her patented cinnamon squash, and your girlfriend ate cranberry sauce for the first time."

Hunter smiled. "They don't have cranberry sauce in Hawaii?"

"I don't know. Maybe she just wasn't brave enough to try it until she came to Cranberry Central. She also had pumpkin pie, which might have been another first."

"Sounds like quite a feast," Hunter said.

Suddenly, his smile seemed forced. There was a sadness in his voice that Jenna had been expecting, but dreading. She reached out and took his hand in hers.

"It was hard, huh?"

He looked up at her and nodded. "To quote you, it pretty much sucked."

"You want to talk about it?"

Hunter went and sat on her bed, and Jenna pulled out her desk chair to sit opposite him. He talked for a while about his mother, whom he loved when she wasn't drinking. There were other relatives, but they were distant—what Melody had once called "holiday relatives." So Hunter had seen most of them on Thanksgiving, and spent the day responding to well-meaning but painful questions about Melody's murder.

"It was awful," he said softly. "But you know, it was worse when they left. With just my mother and me there, it was like the place was haunted. I have so many great memories, the best memories, of that house, but Melody's in every one. I wish my mother would sell it."

"Is she doing any better with it?" Jenna asked, her heart aching for her friend.

Hunter glanced away and swallowed. "She's more haunted than the house," he said quietly.

Jenna hugged him tightly. Hunter returned the embrace.

"I'm so glad to be back," he said, moving back from her slightly. "The weirdest thing is, this is where she died, but . . ." His words trailed off. He looked thoughtful a moment, then started again. "When I was home, everything seemed to remind me that she was dead, how much I miss her. But when I'm back here, everything—you and Yoshiko and Somerset itself—makes me feel like she's still around."

Jenna felt tears welling up and fought them off, wiping her eyes. "I know what you mean," she said. "I miss her so much. Maybe that's why I keep you around."

Hunter looked up at her, shocked. But then Jenna grinned, and they both chuckled softly.

"Thanks," he said.

"Don't mention it." She hugged him again.

There came the sound of a key in the lock, and then Yoshiko opened the door to find the two of them sitting on the edge of the bed, holding each other close.

"Hello?" she said, surprised. "I hope I'm not interrupting anything?"

"Nope," Jenna replied, leaving her arm around Hunter. "Just making time with your man."

"Hi, sweetheart," Hunter said, a bit sheepishly. He stood up and went to give Yoshiko a hug. "We were just talking about Melody. Sharing."

With one eyebrow raised, Yoshiko glared at him. "Well, just don't share too much, mister."

Hunter smiled. "No. That I save all for you."

"Can I just say *eeeew* and get out of here before this gets even more disgusting?" Jenna asked.

Yoshiko and Hunter shared a long kiss and stared into each other's eyes for a few moments, touching. Jenna stood and picked her books up off the floor.

"So!" Yoshiko said, cutting short her reunion interlude with her boyfriend. "Plans tonight?"

"I'm going out with Damon. Redbone's in Lafford Square. You guys are welcome to come along," Jenna offered.

The couple exchanged a glance, and Yoshiko nodded. "We're there."

Redbone's was great. Jenna had barbecued ribs and homemade root beer in a frosted mug. It wasn't the kind of place she'd usually go on a date—ribs were too sloppy to eat in front of someone she wanted to impress—but Damon was different. They were friends first. The date thing was something else entirely.

Which is good, she thought, watching him dig into his side of red beans and rice, and using what must have been her fiftieth napkin to wipe barbecue sauce off her mouth. *'Cause sloppy doesn't even begin to describe it.*

Hunter and Yoshiko were engaged in a conversation all their own. Not that they hadn't participated in the whole group thing, but in the quiet moments, they were getting reacquainted. They'd been apart for four whole days, which, observing their behavior, Jenna realized, had seemed like forever to them.

But right about now, she wasn't thinking much about them. Hunter and Yoshiko seemed to be doing just fine on their own. Jenna's focus was elsewhere.

"Okay, back up," she told Damon. "You're saying Olivia . . . our Olivia, slept with Brick?"

Damon grinned, obviously enjoying her astonishment. "Oh, yeah. And it wasn't any romantic interlude either. They had an SAAL party last weekend, and Brick was hitting on her something fierce, and Olivia got all crazy."

Jenna was a little dubious about that. Olivia Adams

getting "all crazy" didn't seem very likely to her. She was a friend, but just barely. SAAL was the Somerset African-American League, and they could be pretty political. Jenna didn't usually even think about someone's race, and hadn't with Olivia, either. But as soon as Olivia learned that Jenna and Damon were interested in each other, Olivia's attitude toward Jenna had changed considerably. Apparently, she didn't think people should date outside their race.

Which Jenna thought was pretty stupid.

"I'll have to give her a wicked hard time about that," Jenna said, enjoying the gossip. "I mean, I know Anthony's probably a dog, too, but at least he's quiet about it."

"What isn't he quiet about?" Damon asked.

Anthony and Brick were his two best friends on campus, and Jenna liked them both. Brick was a wiseguy, though sweet. He was heavily into the Somerset theater scene, and seemed to have earned a reputation as kind of a dog. Ant, on the other hand, was on the football team, and was about as quiet and polite as guys ever came.

But to Jenna's mind, neither one of them held a candle to Damon Harris. This was round two in their flirtation with dating. The first one had come about mainly out of mutual attraction, and hadn't really gone anywhere. Then they'd become friends, and that led to another try at the romance thing.

Damon was from suburban New Jersey. He was a honey, no doubt, dark and handsome and very confident, which Jenna liked. But beyond that, he was smart and funny and relaxed around women in a way that most men just couldn't manage.

For a long time, she'd had a crush on a local cop named Danny Mariano. Still did. But until recently, she'd let that crush get in the way of her really paying attention to Damon. She was glad she'd finally been able to see past that, which consisted mainly of realizing that she and Danny were an impossible fantasy.

Damon, on the other hand, was very possible. *As for fantasy . . .*

Jenna blushed just looking at him.

"What?" he asked, making a face.

"Nothing," she replied, flustered by her train of thought. "I just . . . I can't believe Olivia, huh? God. What did you say to Brick?"

He looked at her like she was crazy. "What do you think I said? 'Well done, my friend.'"

Mouth open, Jenna stared at him. Then she started to laugh. "You really *are* all pigs, aren't you?"

Damon looked dubious. "This is news?"

Jenna just shook her head and went back to eating her ribs. "Sometimes I don't know about you, Mr. Harris. If I'm going to have a man in my life, I don't want him to be just one of the guys."

"Is that what I am?"

At first, Jenna pretended to ignore him. Then she gave him an evil grin. "Maybe," she said. "But I guess I'll find out as we go along."

She was just looking at him, but this time, he didn't say anything. Instead, Damon's eyes stayed with hers, searching. His smile began to recede as he grew serious. Then he leaned in, slowly, reaching out to slip his left hand around the nape of her neck and draw Jenna close to kiss her.

Jenna's heart beat faster, that indefinable energy between them almost crackling. Her smile became soft. Then she froze.

"Oh, wait—" There was barbecue sauce smeared on her mouth from the ribs. "Sorry to break the moment, but this is so gross." She reached for a napkin.

Chuckling softly, Damon moved in and kissed her anyway. Jenna went to stop him, but then she didn't want to. The humor died away from it, and the kiss went on.

It tasted of barbecue sauce.

Monday was a gray day, sky heavy with the threat of rain all morning. After her Spanish class let out, Jenna went down to her father's apartment for lunch. Frank Logan lived on the first floor of an old house at the edge of campus. It had been a week since they'd last gotten together, even though he was a professor at Somerset. He was working on the second draft of a criminology book that was overdue to the publisher, and had been hiding out again.

Jenna had asked him to come to her mother's house in Natick for Thanksgiving, but her father had passed. He'd spent it with his girlfriend, Shayna Emerson, a wispy English professor whom Jenna liked very much, even though the relationship meant she didn't get to see her father as much.

"Shayna's not here?" she asked as she walked into the apartment.

"Just you and me, kid," Frank told her, smiling.

Jenna frowned. She'd expected Shayna, and her father seemed anxious about something. He said nothing, though, and went right to the kitchen, where he set about making chicken-salad sandwiches with onions and celery while he asked Jenna about Thanksgiving at home, how her mother was doing, and if she was getting ready for finals.

He talked a lot. Much more, in fact, than she was used to from him.

"Dad?" she said, when he brought their plates to the table.

"Do you want pickles?" Frank asked, and turned back to open the refrigerator, rooting around for them before she even answered the question.

"I'm not really in a pickle mood," she replied. "What's wrong?"

He looked at her sheepishly, and then closed the refrigerator. With a little decisive nod, he came to sit across from her and met her gaze. Then he smiled a little nervously.

"I wanted to tell you first," he said.

"Tell me what?" she asked, a bit worried.

"I asked Shayna to marry me."

Jenna stared at him a moment, and then she let out a loud whoop and leaped from her chair. She practically threw herself into her father's arms and gave him a long hug.

"That is the best news!" she said. "Very cool."

"You didn't even ask if she said yes."

With a frown, Jenna punched him in the shoulder. "Of course she said yes!"

"Well, I'm glad it was obvious to you," he said. "But it would have taken some of the pressure off if you'd let me in on it."

Father and daughter hugged again, and then Jenna stood up.

"This is great," she said. "So when's the wedding?"

"Next fall," he said. "We haven't set an exact date yet."

Frank glanced away, gaze darting about the room again. Jenna noticed immediately, but couldn't imagine what could be bothering him now. Shayna was a good match for her dad, though they were opposites in so many ways; he always rumpled, she always perfectly coiffed, she so slim, and he . . . not quite so much.

"There's more?"

He nodded. Took a breath. "I've signed a contract for another book with this publisher. With that, and the wedding coming up, and just being pretty burned out, Shayna and I are both taking a semester sabbatical."

Jenna was waiting for the axe to fall. "So? A few months without teaching. What's the problem?"

"In the south of France."

All through her International Relations class that afternoon, Jenna tried to fool herself into believing she wasn't both hurt and angry. She was genuinely happy for her father, because of both the wedding and his decision to take a sabbatical.

Must be nice, she thought. *Take a semester off, hang out in France for a few months.*

What bothered her, of course, was the France part of

it. She had chosen Somerset because it was an excellent school, and it had a beautiful campus, and it wasn't *too* far from home. The fact that it was where her father taught was just a bonus. As nervous as she'd been at first, Jenna had really enjoyed getting to know her father better. Since her parents had divorced when Jenna was very young, she'd seen him a couple of times a year, if that. This had been a great opportunity for both of them.

Now he's just blowing it off.

Slowly, her anger rose. Jenna knew it was partly because if she got mad, she wouldn't feel the hurt as much. But that was all right with her. Unfortunately, it didn't last. By the time IR class let out, the anger had subsided again, and when she walked back to Sparrow Hall, she just felt sad and abandoned.

Jenna found herself thinking about Slick and Dyson. The former was the medical examiner at Somerset Medical Center, and had been her boss when she worked there. He wasn't a friend, really, he just seemed much too *adult* for that, though he was only in his early forties. Still, he had been so supportive; they'd really bonded. Dyson, on the other hand, really was her friend. He was a pathology resident at SMC, and he and Jenna had kind of a sibling-type relationship going.

Or they had, until she'd bailed from her job. She'd loved the work. It was very rewarding to investigate the cause of a death, to solve a puzzle that might be haunting the loved ones of the deceased. But several times, she'd gotten too involved, and it had put her in danger. It was too much.

She missed it, and even more, she had missed them.

Jenna had felt like she was part of something important when she worked with Slick and Dyson. Every time she glanced over and saw Somerset Medical School and SMC beyond it, she thought about going by to visit, but she never did. Several times, she'd talked to Dyson on the phone. After the first time, he knew better than to ask when she was coming back.

Though she knew never to say never, Jenna didn't really *want* to go back. At least, that's what she kept telling herself.

But she did want to see them. Especially now.

So instead of turning up the short paved walk to Sparrow Hall, she kept on going, past a couple of other dorms, past the quad, and across Carpenter Street. A couple of minutes later, she found herself riding the elevator up to the second-floor administrative wing of Somerset Medical Center, and realized just how much she had missed it.

When she worked here, it had given her purpose and direction. It had made her feel special, in a way that she didn't think most college students ever felt. She had known what she wanted to do with her life, and was already doing it. Helping. Solving. Being on the team. Not that her quitting her job meant she wasn't still planning to go into forensics and pathology. But learning about it just didn't have the same immediacy, the same intensity, as actually doing it.

Which was exactly what I wanted.

Wasn't it?

At the end of the hall, Jenna knocked lightly on the closed door to the Medical Examiner's office, and then went in without waiting for an answer. Dyson was standing by his desk, just hanging up the phone. When he looked up and saw her, a broad smile stretched across his face.

"Jenna!"

Dyson threw his arms around her and hugged her so tightly he nearly lifted her off the ground.

"Can't . . . breathe . . ." she joked.

"What brings you here?" he asked hopefully. "Please tell me you're coming back to work."

"Not this time," she said, smile faltering. "What, I can't come by and say hello?"

With a wistful look, Dyson touched her shoulder tenderly. "Of course you can. How are you, anyway?"

For a second, she almost unloaded on him about her father. It was fresh on her mind and still bothering her. But that wasn't what she had gone up there for, so on second thought, she kept it to herself.

"I'm good," she said. "How are *you* doing?"

"Well, it's been pretty hectic around here in the last couple of weeks. I think you made Slick and I both pretty lazy. Now we're trying to pick up the slack."

Jenna frowned. "He hasn't hired anyone?"

Dyson's eyes ticked toward the door, then back to Jenna. "Honestly? Before you started to work here, he wasn't convinced we really needed a diener. But once you left, well, it became pretty obvious how much we really do. I guess he'll get around to hiring someone new, eventually. But I think he's hoping you'll change your mind."

Though she was tempted to protest again, Jenna

didn't. Instead, she smiled warmly; the idea that Slick needed her, missed her, touched her more than she ever would have imagined. Still, though, the moment she walked into the office she had become resolute. She was done, for now.

"How's Doug?" she asked.

Dyson nodded contentedly. "He's great. Thanks for asking. I think he may be the one, actually."

"I wouldn't have thought you believed in 'the one.' "

"Oh, I think we all do, even if we lie about it. What about you?"

"I'm working on it," Jenna said, and her thoughts went back to her date with Damon the night before. "But I think the search is going well. Anyway, I really only came up here to say hi. Is Slick around?"

Dyson gestured toward the door. "Should be back any second. We have an autopsy to do, but he had a meeting first. If you want to stick around, I'm sure he'd be really happy to see you."

Jenna thought about it, and then shook her head. "Know what? Just tell him I said hi. I'll drop by again."

"You got it, Jenna. Maybe you could come by for lunch one day?"

"That'd be nice," she said.

Just as she turned to go, however, the door was pushed open, and Dr. Slikowski wheeled his chair into the office. Even as he did so, he was speaking.

"All right, Al," he said to Dyson, "let's get this one taken—"

The M.E. spotted Jenna and blinked. He stopped the chair, and for a few seconds, he just looked at her.

"I know," she said awkwardly. "Look what the cat dragged in, huh?"

"Not at all," he said. "I'm very pleased to see you, Jenna. You're just visiting?"

There was a larger question in his words, and they both knew it. Jenna chose to ignore it.

"Yeah," she agreed. "Y'know us teenagers. Young and vibrant, get a little antsy if we go a whole three weeks without seeing a corpse."

Slick tilted his head inquiringly. "Is that so? Well, you're welcome to come down with us, if you like."

"I think I'll pass, but thanks."

"It's nice to see you," Slick said.

"Yeah. You too." Jenna started to leave, but when she was halfway out the door, Dr. Slikowski called her back.

"Well, I know how you thrive on this sort of thing," he said. "I had a call from the M.E. at Mass General earlier that I thought might interest you. Another puzzle."

Just walk out, Jenna told herself. *You don't want to know.*

"What's that?" she asked.

Slick smiled. "They're trying to figure out how a dead man can commit multiple murder."

chapter 2

Castillo felt bad for the grave diggers. When their shovels had first split the dirt in front of Marc Cohen's headstone, the sky had been hanging low and gray, the air saturated and shimmering with that surreal quality that the detective had always thought made such days feel like movie sets instead of real life.

The setting was pretty surreal, too.

Elmwood cemetery wasn't actually in Boston, but in nearby Watertown, which was beyond Castillo's jurisdiction. He'd jumped through hoops to get the exhumation order on Cohen's grave. The judge didn't want to upset Cohen's relatives, or his employers at the *Boston Globe*, by allowing him to be exhumed. Somehow the guy couldn't get it through his head that they weren't exactly exhuming Cohen, since his body was in the morgue at Mass General.

Fortunately, Castillo's lieutenant had reached out to the Watertown P.D. and gotten their backing, so the judge had allowed the exhumation, even though he didn't quite understand it.

Now, though, despite the headache that was spiking dinner forks into both his temples, and the hassle he'd been through just to get here, Castillo didn't feel sorry for himself. He felt bad for the grave diggers instead.

No one should have to dig up dead people in the rain, he thought. *Or at all, for that matter.*

The rain had been falling steadily for twenty minutes and showed no sign of letting up. If anything it was coming down harder, and the wind was picking up, driving it down at an angle. Already, the two men down in the grave—they could only use mechanical equipment at the beginning, to avoid the risk of damaging the casket—had their hair plastered against their scalps by the rain.

Castillo had an umbrella in his trunk, but he didn't dare get it. It wouldn't do the diggers any good, and if he used it, they might just bury him down there in Cohen's place.

"Hell of a day for this," grumbled Gary Fox, the detective with the Watertown P.D. who'd drawn the short straw and had to suffer along with Castillo and the diggers.

"You can wait in the car, Detective," Castillo said. "I won't tell."

Fox glared at him. Castillo had been trying to lighten up the situation, but apparently the other cop didn't appreciate his efforts. Not at all.

"What are you expecting to find down there?" Fox

asked. "You got the guy's corpse already. You think it's empty?"

Castillo wiped rain from his face and looked at the other man. Of course he thought it was empty, but he wasn't going to express his expectations in case they were wrong. It might have been a life insurance scam, or that he wanted to leave his wife . . . it could have been just about anything. But he'd been down that investigative route already. Cohen had died of a massive systemwide failure of bodily functions and an apparent heart attack in a hospital in front of four witnesses, including his wife and the man who'd been his doctor for seven years.

When Castillo had questioned the doctor, asked him how certain he was that Cohen was dead, the man had glared at him.

"If he'd been shot through the head in my presence, I wouldn't be any more certain," the man had said. "You say he was walking around for a month after, and I say that's impossible."

"So we're talking a miracle?" Castillo had replied dubiously.

"Or a mysterious twin, separated at birth," the doctor had said. "But that only happens on daytime television. Or the Jerry Springer show."

"You watch too much TV."

"Don't we all?"

Thinking back on it now, Castillo found himself amused by the doctor's attitude. It was impossible. That much was true. But that didn't make it any less real.

Thunkk!

"Got it," one of the diggers said, from down in the grave.

"Thank God," Gary Fox muttered.

A short time later, the casket was lifted out of the hole. Before Castillo could even bend to look at it, the diggers had their say.

"Don't feel empty," one of them said.

"Still sealed," replied the other.

They were right. The casket was heavy.

"Open it," Castillo said.

The diggers looked at him. "Sorry," one of them mumbled. "That ain't in the job description."

Fox also balked. "You're taking it for evidence. Why don't you bring it back to Boston and open it there?"

Castillo looked at him without expression. "Don't you want to know?" he asked.

Fox looked down at the diggers. "Open it up," he said.

Swearing, the men used the edges of their shovels to pry the casket open. It didn't take very long. When they were done, Castillo got down and lifted the lid.

The stink was horrid and he recoiled slightly, backing away and letting the lid drop.

"No vacancy," Castillo said.

"So if your DOA at Mass General is Marc Cohen, then who's this guy?" Fox asked.

"We'll see," Castillo replied. "We will definitely see."

Jenna was torn. As she stood there and listened to Slick provide the details about the apparent resurrection of Marc Cohen and his subsequent turn to the dark side of the Force, she knew she ought to just leave. It wasn't her job anymore. She didn't want it to be.

But she couldn't resist a puzzle. Slick had been right about that.

"So there was no autopsy?" she asked. "The first time, I mean."

Dyson chuckled slightly at that, shaking his head. "Y'know Jenna, I wonder if it's you," he said. "I mean, this is never a happy-go-lucky job. It's ugly. People die in some truly horrible ways, not even counting murder. But whenever you're around, things just seem to get weirder."

Jenna shot him a withering glance. "Gee, thanks."

Slick cleared his throat. Despite the fact that he was in a wheelchair, placing him well below eye level when he was speaking with people who were standing, he usually controlled the conversation by his presence alone. Which never stopped Dyson from putting his two cents in, sarcastic though they often were.

"In answer to your question, Jenna," Slick said, arching an admonishing eyebrow in Dyson's direction, "Mr. Cohen died of an apparent heart attack, in the hospital, under supervision. There was no need to perform an autopsy at that time."

"But he was buried, right? Which means embalming, right? How do you get up and walk away from that?"

Slick smiled warmly at Jenna. "How indeed," he said. "It's nice to see you, Jenna. Even if it's only a visit. I do wish you'd come by more often, though."

Jenna was slightly taken aback by the change of subject. But then Slick's smile faded a bit.

"The Boston police are looking into it, of course. Obviously the man was never embalmed, though how that happened, I can't imagine. It might have been some sort of scam, though how that led to a reporter with an impeccable reputation robbing and killing a small crowd of drug dealers is beyond my imagination. It will be interesting to find out, however."

Slick looked at Dyson. "I suppose we should get on with it, Al," he said. "Don't want to keep the customers waiting." Then he smiled at Jenna again. "I'm sorry to abandon you, Jenna. You're welcome to join us for this autopsy, if you like."

"Thanks, but I'll pass," she said, her mind still going over the conversation about Marc Cohen.

With a nod, Slick looked at Dyson. "Would you mind grabbing that Coltrane CD off my desk?"

"Got it," Dyson said and went into Dr. Slikowski's inner office.

Which was when Slick surprised Jenna. He turned to look at her again, almost gravely this time.

"We miss you around here, you know," the M.E. said. "Dyson and I both do. You know I admire your natural inquisitiveness, and your persistence, and the fact that you often look at things in ways other people miss. I'd started to see you as a protégée, of sorts, I suppose. I know you have a long road ahead of you before such a thing could actually happen, but you did help us a great deal, and the police as well. If you ever change your mind, let me know."

It was very awkward. At first, Jenna didn't know what to say. But then she knew what she *had* to say.

"You don't know how much I appreciate that, Dr. Slikowski," she said. "But I just can't—"

"I know," he said. "And I'm not asking you to. It was only that I didn't tell you these things before you left. Not really. And I thought you should hear it."

Dyson poked his head out of the inner office. "Are you sure the Coltrane's on your desk?" he asked.

Slick smiled. "Not completely, no. Forget it. Maybe it's downstairs."

Dyson shrugged, and then the three of them left the office together. They went down the hall to the elevator. Riding down, Jenna pressed L, and Dyson hit B for the basement. That part felt strange, too. A part of her felt that she ought to be going down there with them. But when the doors parted on the first floor, she gave Dyson's hand a squeeze and then stepped off.

"Great to see you," he said.

"Come see us again, Jenna," Slick added. "Remember, there's always a place for you here."

Jenna didn't have a reply for that, so she was silent as the doors closed. When the elevator had moved on, she walked thoughtfully out the front doors of the hospital and along the paved path that led back onto the Somerset campus.

Between Slick's words and the mystery of what had happened to Marc Cohen, she had a lot to think about. For nearly ten minutes, she'd forgotten all about the fact that her father was taking off for France.

By the time she got back to Sparrow Hall, however, she was thinking once more about her father's impending departure. She was still sad about it, but a lot of her anger had dissipated.

Jenna walked up to room 311 and found the door unlocked. She went in, expecting Yoshiko, but found herself alone. With a frown, she checked her answering machine. There was only one message, from her mother.

"Hi, sweetie," the machine said, in April Blake's voice. "I talked to your father earlier. He told me you were a little upset about him going away. Why don't you give me a call?"

As usual, she had predicted Jenna's reaction to the news. After a moment's hesitation, Jenna called her. Her mother was glad to hear from her. Though April had once been married to Frank Logan, she seemed genuinely pleased to hear that he was going to remarry. Jenna was happy about that, because she liked Shayna too.

But her mother also understood perfectly her anger about the sabbatical to Europe. It didn't take Jenna long to realize that April was almost as angry as she was.

In the midst of their conversation, Jenna heard someone trying the door. Then there was a knock. She walked over and pulled it open to find Yoshiko standing in the hall with a pair of large leafy potted plants in her arms.

"Hang on, Mom," Jenna said, then she looked accusingly at Yoshiko. "You left the door unlocked."

Yoshiko blinked in surprise. "Just watering the plants. I didn't want to have to get out my keys."

Jenna nodded, feeling silly for making a deal out of it. She hoped her facial expression communicated the appropriate self-recrimination. Just in case, she covered the phone.

"Sorry," she said in a low voice. "Bad day."

Yoshiko nodded and went about putting the plants back in their usual spots.

"Listen, Mom, I should go. But don't worry. I'll deal," Jenna said. "It isn't like he's been chaperoning me around."

"I know that, honey," April said. "But he promised he'd look after you. That he'd try to make a new start as a father."

"It's a little late for that," Jenna said sharply.

Her mother paused a second. Jenna could hear her breathing on the phone.

"I'm not really helping, am I?" April asked at length.

"Weirdly enough, you are," Jenna told her. "I have gotten closer to him, but it isn't like one semester away is the biggest deal in the world. I'm good right where I am. I'm a big girl, y'know?"

"You don't have to remind me." April sighed.

Jenna chuckled. "I'll be okay," she said, just before she hung up the phone. "I'll be fine."

"God, what a mess."

Danny Mariano and his partner, Audrey Gaines, stood in the midst of a sea of shattered glass that had once been Pappas Jewelers. It had been in the Pappas family for three generations, located in the same spot in Lafford Square for more than sixty years. According to Theo Pappas, the current manager, the store had been robbed before, but never anything like this.

No one had ever been killed before.

"Guy was a bull in a china shop," Audrey muttered to Danny, so that the other members of the crime scene team—and Mr. Pappas—wouldn't hear her. "Had to be flying to do all this damage. It wasn't even necessary."

Danny looked around. She was right about that. Before making Somerset's homicide unit, he'd been in robbery. He'd seen a lot of thefts, from convenience stores and private homes to jewelry stores and banks. But Pappas Jewelers was a hell of a mess.

Most of the display cases had been shattered, as had the glass doors, which had been locked. The gate, on the other hand, had been down, but not locked.

Not locked because Lois Pappas, Theo's mother, had been doing the books in the back room at the time.

Now she lay in the center of the room, her face a pulpy mess of blood and bone fragments. The crime scene photographer was taking his shots now, and soon they'd bag her up and carry her out. When the burglar had come in, smashing and grabbing anything that sparkled, Mrs. Pappas had reached into the office safe and pulled out a gun that her son had left there for that purpose.

If she'd waited, Danny thought, *she might have had a chance at the guy.*

But Mrs. Pappas hadn't waited for him in the office. She went out to face him, tried to shoot, but apparently missed her target. For her trouble, she was bludgeoned to death with a brass coatrack that had stood by the door.

"Mostly diamonds," Danny said aloud.

Audrey turned to look at him. "What?"

He waved a hand to take in the destruction. "It's a hell of a mess, and it sure looks like a smash-and-grab. But the perp took mostly diamonds. Rings. Tennis bracelets. Earrings."

His partner frowned. "How can you tell just standing there?"

"Been in too many jewelry stores, maybe." He offered a small shrug. "Take a look around. You'll see it, too."

Before Audrey could respond, one of the uniforms on scene, a guy named Vin Delmonico, walked up to Danny, glancing around nervously.

"What've you got?" Danny asked. "You get a statement from the owner?"

Delmonico nodded. "We're set with that. I just was wondering, if you guys are gonna want to question him, if maybe you can do it somewhere else. Looks like it'll be a little while yet before the body's moved, and maybe he shouldn't have to see his mother like that."

Danny glanced over at Theo Pappas, who stood in a corner drinking a cup of coffee one of the officers had given him, doing everything he could not to look at his mother's corpse. Though he was only in his forties, Pappas looked frail. It was common sense for them to consider him a suspect. He'd known that the gate would be unlocked, that his mother would be there alone, and with all the damage . . . well, it was certainly possible that the robbery was to cover up the murder, not the other way around.

But Danny didn't think so. Not with someone going to the trouble of focusing on the diamonds. Plus Pappas looked genuinely aggrieved, not skittish the way perps usually looked when they were trying to cover up that they'd offed a loved one.

"Tell him to go home," Danny said. "We'll pay him a visit shortly."

Delmonico nodded, obviously pleased with the response. It was clear to Danny that Officer Delmonico didn't think Theo Pappas was their guy either. He'd have to keep an eye on Delmonico, the man had good instincts.

When he turned his attention back to the crime scene, he saw that Audrey was talking to Darren Chomsky, the head crime scene tech. He wanted to listen in, but something else caught his attention. As Audrey spoke to Chomsky, Danny made a quick circuit of the store, looking carefully at the way things were broken, the spray of the glass, and the blood that spattered the floor around Mrs. Pappas's corpse.

"Audrey," he said.

When she didn't respond, he looked up. She held up a finger, indicating she needed a moment with Chomsky. Then she nodded and walked over to where he stood.

"What's up with Chomsky?" he asked.

"In a second," she said. "What've you got?"

Danny nodded down at a splatter of blood among the glass shards and on the broken case in front of them.

"What do you make of this?"

Audrey studied the blood, then glanced over her shoulder at the dead woman. When she looked back at him, Danny pointed at a spot on the floor, nearer the door.

"And that."

She walked over and crouched by it, then looked back at the blood on the case.

"Chomsky!" she called.

Audrey looked up at Danny, and he nodded as Chomsky came over.

"Looks like our perp cut himself," she said, pointing at the drops of blood on the floor. Already, somebody had walked on it. Maybe several somebodies, even the perp himself. "This should match the blood on that broken case back there."

"But not the DOA," Danny clarified.

Chomsky nodded and gestured to one of his techs to come over and get a sample.

"So, prints?" Danny asked.

Chomsky looked at Audrey. "As I just told Detective Gaines," the man said, "it's a retail place. It'd probably be impossible to get effective prints off any of the glass or the door or gate."

"There's a 'but' coming, isn't there?" Danny said. Chomsky hadn't mentioned gloves, which meant he knew the perp hadn't been wearing any. "What've you got?"

"Murder weapon," Chomsky said. "It isn't likely anybody's actually picked the thing up in a while. But we lifted a couple of very clear prints off it."

Danny glanced quickly over at the brass coatrack. The crime scene guys had stood it back up, and even now were wrapping it in plastic. Then his eyes went to the dead woman again, even as a body bag was laid down beside her. It was a horrible crime. Disgustingly brutal.

When he looked at Audrey, he saw that she was as furious as he was.

"I'll call you as soon as I have something," Chomsky added.

"Do that," Audrey said. "Thanks, Darren."

Chomsky nodded and went back to directing his team. After he'd walked away, Danny glanced at his partner again.

"Who the hell would do something like this, even if it *was* just a smash-and-grab, without wearing gloves?" he asked.

Audrey looked around the store and shook her head. "Hell if I know," she said. "But if those prints come up anywhere, we're going to find out."

Danny took one last look at Mrs. Pappas's ruined face, right before they zipped her into the body bag. Then he turned to follow Audrey out of the store, so they could go question the woman's son as a suspect in her murder.

Neither one of them believed Theo Pappas had anything to do with it. But they couldn't be sure.

That was the job.

chapter 3

It was only a few days after Thanksgiving, but already Boston was decorated for Christmas. Huge wreaths adorned the sides of buildings and hung from lampposts. Every store was strung with lights or ribbons and garlands. On Boston Common, the trees were dotted with white bulbs, and an ice rink had been created where the swans glided in the summertime.

Throughout the city, bells rang, some from sidewalk Santas, and others from church steeples. In the theater district, people began to gather after dinner, forming lines for the most popular of shows.

Somewhere, voices were raised in song. "Silver Bells."

Wrapped in a wool sweater and her soft brown leather jacket, Jenna looked around in wonder.

"Is it me, or does Christmas come a little earlier every year?"

Damon offered a small smile in return. "It's you," he

said. "I kind of like it. As freezing as it gets, all the holiday glitter makes it seem not so cold."

"Speak for yourself," Jenna replied, shivering a little and shoving her hands deep in the pockets of her jacket.

Without hesitation, Damon slipped an arm around her and held her beside him as they walked. Jenna didn't mind at all. It felt nice, and natural, for him to have his arm around her.

It was Tuesday night, and Damon had surprised her that morning by suggesting they go into Boston. He wanted to take her to his favorite restaurant, and there was a kind of gleam in his eye that Jenna couldn't resist.

Which was how they found themselves walking down Stuart Street a little before seven o'clock that night. They'd taken the T in from Somerset, and a short walk brought them to a Japanese steak house called Kyoto. When they reached the door, Damon held it open for her.

"You're going to love this," he said.

Somehow, she trusted him. It was a little strange for Jenna to find herself feeling that way. She still had a bit of a crush on Danny Mariano, a detective with the Somerset P.D. But when it became obvious that wasn't going to go anywhere, she'd known she had to move on. She liked Damon. Always had. But she had never expected to find herself liking him as much as she did.

Looking at him in that moment, smiling so gallantly as he held the door open, and remembering how comfortable it had been with his arm around her, Jenna felt a tiny alarm bell go off within her. *Careful, girl,* she thought. *Dangerous.*

It would be all too easy for her to love Damon Harris.

Though their reservation was for seven o'clock, the hostess told them there would be a short wait, and they went into the lounge. They were both under twenty-one, but Jenna was still a bit surprised that Damon didn't even try to order alcohol. A lot of guys would have tried to fake it. To some, in a twisted way, drinking was a sign of maturity. Jenna thought people like that were sad. They never realized that it was exactly that belief that made them immature.

But Damon was nothing like that. Though he had his "guy" moments with Anthony and Brick, he seemed content in his own skin, yet without being arrogant.

Well, maybe a little arrogant, Jenna thought. But in moderation, she found arrogance kind of attractive.

While they waited, she glanced deeper into the restaurant and saw a sign that read "Sushi Bar." Instantly, her stomach did a little flip.

"Please don't tell me you brought me here to eat sushi," she said, slightly panicked, and a little embarrassed. " 'Cause, I'm sorry, I don't eat anything that hasn't been cooked first."

"No, no. You'll like this. Very cooked. Right in front of you, in fact."

Jenna frowned, not understanding for a second. Then she got it. "This is one of those places where the table is actually the stove," she said, trying to get a clearer look into the dining area.

"You've been to one?" Damon asked.

"Never," she said. "I guess as long as none of the knives go flying and impale me, it'll be interesting."

Damon laughed. "Actually, I did see the chef let go of a big wooden salt shaker one time. It flew out of his hand and smashed this guy's wineglass. Red wine, tan pants. Not a pretty combination."

"But I bet he got his meal for free," Jenna said optimistically.

Several minutes later, they were led back into the restaurant proper, where several dining rooms, each with four large tables, were set apart from one another. Jenna and Damon were seated at the end of one table. An older couple sat across from them, and a group of women, who appeared to be celebrating something, sat along one of the long sides of the table.

There were no chairs on the fourth side. In fact, the table itself was a sheet of metal, surrounded by a strip of wood perhaps eighteen inches wide, save for that one side, where the metal went all the way to the edge. Jenna thought it was odd to sit at a table in a nice restaurant with a bunch of people that she didn't know, but that was obviously part of the experience.

The menu was fairly simple. Fish, shrimp, beef, chicken, pork, lots of vegetables, rice and soup, with everything but the soup cooked right on the table. Jenna and Damon decided to share their meals, and ended up with a little bit of everything.

After the waitress took their orders, the chef came into the room, trundling a cart laden with cutlery and wooden salt and pepper shakers, among other things, to the table. He turned on the heat to the stove, and then introduced himself in heavily accented English. Almost immediately, he began to cook some very crisp, fresh-looking vegetables, with a little bit of sesame oil.

"Suddenly I'm incredibly hungry," Jenna told Damon in a low voice.

Moments later, the waitress brought a salad with ginger dressing, which was followed by a delicious soup. While they were eating their soup, the chef began to cook a shrimp appetizer, sprinkled with sesame seeds. They had each been given a little dish of mustard sauce and another sauce Jenna hadn't caught the name of, and when the shrimp came off the stove, she dipped it in each sauce and found them delicious.

Watching the chef work, first on the shrimp, and then on the meat and fish that were brought out for the entrées of those at the table, was the real treat. Knives flashed and spun, cutting, organizing, and delivering food to plates. Wooden salt and pepper shakers clacked together.

Somewhere in the midst of all that, Damon reached out for Jenna's hand, twined his fingers in her own, and held on. She squeezed back, almost without thinking of it, and they sat like that, enjoying the show. When all the food had been delivered to the appropriate plates, they applauded along with everyone else.

Everything she tasted was fresh and delicious.

And the company was wonderful. She and Damon talked about classes, and about their plans for the Christmas break—she was going to be home with her mother, but Damon's family had planned a trip to Captiva Island in Florida for the week after the holiday, and Jenna was jealous. They talked about her job, why she'd quit and the slight temptation to go back that she felt from time to time.

Damon admitted that he was glad she'd quit. Not that it wasn't fascinating, but she'd put herself in danger a couple of times, and he thought she was probably better off.

Part of Jenna wanted to argue, but she couldn't.

What she didn't talk about was her father, his upcoming wedding and the sabbatical he was taking. She was having a sweet, romantic night, and she didn't want to spoil it for either of them by talking about things that would only make her sad.

The perfect night, really. Damon had been right; she loved the restaurant. There was an atmosphere to it that was entirely unique. And then there was Damon's smile, the way he looked at her. Jenna liked that very much. It didn't feel like the kind of date she usually had, to the movies or to Pizzeria Uno, or something. It felt like more than that.

Which was why she felt so horribly guilty. Time and time again over the course of the night, she found her mind wandering to Danny Mariano, wondering what he was doing, and what it might have been like to have such a date with him. It wasn't fair to Damon, she knew that. And she liked Damon, very much. She really felt there was something happening between them. But she knew that before that could happen, she had to get Danny out of her system completely. She'd thought she had, but apparently that wasn't the case.

Jenna worked hard at pushing thoughts of him away, at focusing on Damon.

"You seem distracted," Damon said when they were halfway through the meal. "What's on your mind?"

Reluctantly, Jenna shrugged. "I told you before about the stuff with my father. I'm just still a little hurt by that, I guess," she said.

Damon squeezed her hand. "You've got plenty of friends," he said. "And more than enough to keep you busy. In fact, I'm hoping to keep you pretty busy all by myself."

Jenna smiled shyly.

"This is nice," Damon added.

"Yeah, it is."

"Not just the date," he went on. "I mean, I like being with you in general, sure, but this is different. Away from campus, and the way we're supposed to act there, y'know? Parties and dining-hall diplomacy and all that. It's nice to spend some time just you and me."

Which was when Jenna felt a little flutter in her heart, and she forgot all about Danny, at least for a while. She leaned forward and kissed Damon, and again felt her heart skip a beat. The kiss was brief, but intense, and when she pulled back, slightly embarrassed, she saw that his eyebrows were raised in surprise.

"Sorry," she muttered.

Damon laughed. "Oh yeah," he said, in mock consternation. "Don't you *dare* do *that* again."

Something changed after that kiss. Simple as that. She sat a little closer to him, searched his eyes more when he talked. On Damon's part, he reached for her hand more, brushed her hair from her eyes.

On the way home, they held hands for the entire duration of the ride on the T, and then walking back from the station to campus. Jenna knew there was something a little old-fashioned about it, but she didn't feel at all self-conscious.

By the time they reached Sparrow Hall, she had come to a somewhat startling realization.

Damon Harris was her boyfriend.

Despite the crisp, clear weather of the night before, Wednesday morning began cold and gray, with the threat of icy rain hanging overhead. The heater in Jason Castillo's Plymouth rattled as he drove out to Watertown. Marc Cohen had been buried out of Katz Funeral Home, and the more he thought about it, the more Castillo figured that David Greenspan was the man he needed to talk to. Greenspan, the director of the funeral home, was the son-in-law of the owner, Leo Katz, whose family had started the business during the Second World War.

But Katz was retired now, and Greenspan was the only guy who got hands-on with his "customers." He was the only one who could give Castillo the answers he needed.

It was shortly after nine A.M. when Castillo pulled up in front of the funeral home. He was always slightly unnerved by such places, classic old homes, as perfectly preserved, with their gleaming paint and manicured lawns, as the corpses for which they served as way station before interment.

There was always something ominous about them.

Castillo went up the front walk. Only moments after

he rapped on the door, it was opened by a smiling blond man in his thirties.

"Detective Castillo?" the man asked.

"You're David Greenspan?"

"That's me," Greenspan replied. "Come on in. Unfortunately, we have a funeral to prepare for, but that's the business. I'm happy to answer any questions you might have, though. What brings you out from Boston?"

Castillo narrowed his eyes as he followed Greenspan in through the funeral home to the man's business office. Once there, he was surprised to find how unlike an office it seemed. There was a desk, true, but other than that, it seemed to be made for comfort, the surroundings pleasant. *But then,* Castillo thought, *it must be important for the people who come in to make arrangements for the burial of a loved one to have pleasant surroundings.*

Despite that comfort zone, however, it was obvious that Greenspan was nervous. He was smiling too much—something not uncommon for people who worked around those who were grieving—but he was also talking a lot.

Castillo sat in a plush leather chair across from Greenspan's desk and folded his hands on his lap, but said nothing.

"So," Greenspan prodded after a few seconds. "You said you had questions for me. How can I help?"

For a moment longer, Castillo held his tongue. Greenspan shifted nervously.

"It's about Marc Cohen," Castillo told the man. "He's dead."

Greenspan blinked, then offered a small nod. "I should hope he's dead," the man said. "We buried him." A tiny smile flickered nervously at the corners of the man's mouth. "Sorry," he said. "That was a little joke. Of course I know that Mr. Cohen is dead. His family, as I'm sure you know or you wouldn't be here, used our services for his burial."

Castillo studied Greenspan for several seconds. "Are you telling me you hadn't heard that we exhumed the body buried in his plot?"

"No," Greenspan said, frowning. "I hadn't heard that. And frankly, I'm surprised his family would allow it. They're quite orthodox, you know."

"Well, they didn't have that much choice," Castillo informed him. "See, we had to figure out if there actually was someone down in that grave."

"What is that supposed to mean, Detective?" Greenspan asked, a bit self-righteously. "I was there. I saw Marc Cohen lowered into the ground."

"Did you see him buried?"

With a sort of wince, Greenspan shook his head. "Well, not really, no. But I know that he was."

"Somebody was," Castillo said. "But it wasn't Marc Cohen. In fact, Cohen only died a couple days ago, and then it was bullets that took him down. He's still at the morgue. Now that we've spoken, I suspect you'll be getting a call. The family's been very anxious to bury him, but given the circumstances, we've had to get them to hold off."

The detective found Greenspan's wide eyes and gaping jaw very gratifying somehow.

"That's—"

"Impossible," Castillo finished. "Yeah. I've been told that. Problem is, it's true."

"I prepared Mr. Cohen for interment myself. His family viewed the body before the funeral."

"Was he embalmed?" Castillo asked.

"Of course not," Greenspan replied, frowning. "Orthodox Jews do not embalm their dead, Detective Castillo. The law allows twenty-four hours for the deceased to be buried without embalming, as long as certain precautions are taken."

"Such as?" Castillo asked.

"Well, only the family can view the deceased," Greenspan noted. "Also, there is a very powerful topical disinfectant that must be applied."

Castillo thought about it. "Cohen didn't have an autopsy," he said. "And he wasn't embalmed. How the hell did you know for certain he was dead?"

Greenspan leaned back in his chair, glaring at Castillo. "I'm afraid I have to take that as an insult, Detective," he said. "Not only had Massachusetts General declared him legally dead, but I have seen enough corpses in my life to know whether a person is alive or dead."

"Great," Castillo said. "So maybe you can explain how it is that your dead man was shooting at me the other day."

But Greenspan couldn't answer that.

Jenna had a Spanish headache on Wednesday afternoon. She knew she wasn't really prepared for the final,

51

so she was studying Spanish verb conjugation. It wasn't fun.

A little more of this and my ears will bleed, she thought.

So when the phone rang, a wave of relief swept over her. She didn't care who it was. Even Yoshiko's mother, who was a little overprotective, would have been a welcome interruption at that point. Jenna would talk her ear off, and then use the excuse that there was so little of the afternoon left to blow off Spanish for the rest of the day. She'd never looked forward to dining hall food more in her life.

On the third ring, she picked up the phone.

But it wasn't Yoshiko's mom. It was Danny Mariano.

"Hey," Jenna said, trying to hide her surprise. "How are you?"

"I'm good," he replied. "A little crazy, as usual. How are you?"

"Also good," she told him. "Really good, actually."

"I'm glad to hear that," Danny said. "I just hadn't talked to you in a while, and I wanted to check in. You must be getting ready for finals now, huh?"

"Well, I'm supposed to be," she admitted, relaxing now, though the sound of his voice had made her a bit nervous at first. "Procrastinating is more like it. I'm just distracted today."

Which was the understatement of the year. Her mind had been very much on Damon all day. Things had gone so well with him the night before, she had finally felt as though she had been able to put her crush on Danny behind her.

Sort of important, considering I have a boyfriend now.

So, of course, Danny picks now to call.

"I talked to Al Dyson last week," he said. "He told me they're suffering over there without you. Given any thought to going back?"

"Not really," she lied. "I think I've hung up my lab coat until medical school." After a pause, she went on. "I did go by there, though. Slick tried roping me in with the latest oddball case. Some guy kills a bunch of drug dealers, then the Boston P.D. has to shoot him. It turns out he was supposed to have died a month earlier, witnesses, a funeral, the whole thing."

There was silence on the other end of the line.

"Danny?" she asked.

"You're sure about this?" His voice sounded different, strained.

"Well, I don't work there anymore, but pretty sure, yeah. Why, what's up?"

The second Jenna asked, a part of her balked. She didn't want to know. She really, really didn't want to know. Just from the tone of his voice, she knew there was more to it, another weird one, and she didn't want to be intrigued, didn't want to be tempted to poke her nose into it.

"We had a robbery-homicide the other day," he said. "Clear prints on the murder weapon, and fresh. But they belonged to a guy named Adam Shefts."

"Problem?" Jenna asked.

"Shefts died six weeks ago."

The inside of the car was a mess. Empty bottles, fast-food containers, porn magazines. He drank, he ate, and he looked at pictures of naked girls. There was very little left in his mind now.

Very little left *of* his mind.

He sat behind the wheel of a rusting Chevy Corsica whose undercarriage squealed miserably whenever he took a left turn. He never noticed the sound. It never occurred to him to take the car in for service. Gas. That was what the car needed. Just as he needed food and liquor and porn, the car needed gas.

It was parked now, and that was good. It was hard to focus while he was driving. Just the day before, he'd gotten a little too far to the right, and scraped the rearview mirrors off two cars that were parked on University Boulevard in Somerset.

He wasn't in Somerset now, though.

He was in Boston.

Boston was nice.

The window was down, though it was very cold. He didn't mind the cold so much. Didn't really notice, actually. The Southern Comfort helped with that, but it wasn't just the whiskey. He didn't notice much of anything, except what he focused on. What he *had* to focus on. And even then, his head hurt.

Like now.

He ate from a giant bag of French fries from Wendy's, and drank the soda he'd spiked with Southern Comfort, and he watched the front door of the building across the street very carefully.

The building. Lots of cops around that building. A police station, that was it, of course.

Of course.

And the man . . . the man is a cop.

Even as he thought of it, the cop came out the front door and walked along the sidewalk to where he'd parked his car. The cop didn't wear a uniform. He was a different kind of cop. He got in his car and drove away.

Focusing, Adam Shefts turned the key in the ignition, put his Chevy in gear, and followed Jason Castillo.

All the way home.

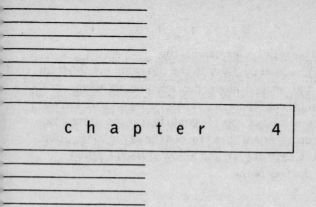

chapter 4

Jace? Hey, you feeling all right? You look like hell."

"That's about right," Castillo replied with a grimace.

Dreadful bubblegum pop music pumped from the den down the hall, and his head throbbed along with the electronic drums. It was Friday night, his niece Miranda's thirteenth birthday, and Castillo wouldn't have missed it for the world. But now he was wondering if he should have stayed home. He felt feverish, and nauseous, and his body had started to ache all over.

He'd taken three Advil, but the aches had only gotten worse. For the moment, he was taking a short break from the party, sitting on the stairs, trying to catch his breath, which seemed to be getting harder and harder to do. Castillo had just decided that he really ought to go home when his brother-in-law, Antoine, had spotted him on the stairs and come over to state the obvious.

"Jace?"

"I think I'm gonna go, Antoine," he mumbled,

though with the fever, his words sounded a bit slurred to him. "Tell Miranda I said good-bye."

Antoine started to argue, but Castillo stood up, almost forcing the man out of his way. He had never liked Antoine, and had never tried to hide that fact from his sister, Helena. But there wasn't any real animosity there. It would be a shame if he had to throw up on his sister's husband.

"Gotta go," he mumbled, and started for the door, wincing at the pounding of the drums.

Antoine clapped a hand on his shoulder and spun him around, peering at him critically.

"What's wrong with you, Jason? Are you drunk?"

Castillo frowned. "I'm sick, Antoine. Going home. Leave me alone."

"You're in bad shape, Jace. Maybe I should drive you," Antoine suggested.

Castillo found himself almost absurdly touched by the suggestion, but he wasn't about to let his niece's father disappear during her birthday party just to drive him home because he felt like death warmed over.

"I'll be okay," he said, trying to force the slur from his voice. "Tell Helena I'll call her tomorrow, okay?"

With that, Antoine gave up. Castillo was relieved. He waved good-bye to several relatives and friends of the family on his way out, and then he was slipping into the soft, comfortable familiarity of his car. For a few seconds, he just sat in the driver's seat, hands gripping the steering wheel, breathing. Just breathing.

If only it was that simple, he thought.

Breathing was suddenly becoming a luxury. It wasn't

that he was congested; at least, it didn't feel that way. Instead, it felt as though his chest was freezing up. In fact, his whole body felt as though it was growing sluggish.

Go home, take massive amounts of drugs, call in sick in the morning, he told himself, already thinking of the NyQuil/Benadryl/Alleve cocktail he'd have to whip up before dropping into bed.

"One way to avoid working Saturday," he told himself.

Castillo started the car and drove along back roads to High Street, which would take him away from Medford and back, eventually, to Boston. He clicked on the radio and was distressed to find the same annoying bubblegum pop that had been playing at the party. Surprised, he glanced down at the radio and saw that it was tuned to a station he almost never listened to. It certainly wasn't preset.

With a frown, he punched a button to get to the River, a station he liked because it played such a variety of music. But when he pulled his hand back, all the tiny bones in his fingers and knuckles seemed to grind together at once, cramping up, and pain spiked up his arm.

"Jesus!" Castillo grunted and swerved onto the other side of the street.

A car horn blared, but Castillo was already acting. He spun the wheel back the other way. Then, when he was safely on his own side of the street, he slammed on the brakes. He didn't put the car in Park because he didn't dare try to use his right hand unless he had to. Instead, he held the hand up in front of his face, wincing as he tried to flex it. It moved, but painfully, and slowly.

Yet the pain was receding. The hand seemed to be growing numb.

God, am I having a heart attack? he thought. Pain in his arm and numbness . . . but his chest didn't hurt. Castillo didn't have a clue what was going on, what was happening to him.

But he knew it was serious.

His breathing growing even more ragged, he glanced over his shoulder, waited for the traffic to clear, and then pulled a U-turn and headed back into the Lawrence Estates area of Medford. He hadn't been there in a couple of years, but he managed to find his way to Lawrence Memorial Hospital. The world seemed to grow hazy around him, like it was all nothing but a mirage. When he parked the car, he struck the side of a van in the next spot, and barely noticed.

Castillo stumbled into the emergency room, his body wracked with pain and fever. When the duty nurse asked him what was wrong, and he opened his mouth to answer, no words came out. Instead, he started coughing. It bent him double, but he couldn't stop. He wheezed, trying to catch his breath, his throat felt dry as splintered wood.

He was surrounded by several people, doctors or nurses or orderlies, he couldn't tell. They were talking to him, trying to get answers, trying to help, but Castillo couldn't talk. The coughing intensified, and then finally began to subside a little.

Then it wracked him again, but it wasn't dry anymore. Bloody spittle sprayed from his throat and spattered the tile floor. Jason Castillo wept as it happened again, and he forced himself to calm down, forced himself to get control of the coughing.

Someone had a needle, and it slipped into his arm with a pinch. A few seconds later, the world started to go away, and he was on a table, and someone was trying to slip a tube into his throat.

Castillo knew that he was dying.

A short time later, however, he was astonished to find himself still alive. He didn't know how much time had passed, but he was in a room, and he could hear voices and other noises out in the hall.

Castillo tried to move his head and found that it took some serious concentration. Even glancing sideways was a chore. There was a mask over his face, feeding him oxygen, and he had some kind of IV set up next to the bed. There was a woman in the room with him. She was short, with reddish blond hair, and she seemed to be studying his chart, or something that was on a clipboard in front of her.

"Hello?" he said, voice muffled by the mask.

The woman looked up instantly, obviously surprised. "Mr. Castillo? Welcome back. I'm Dr. Wheeler."

"What the hell's . . ." he managed to croak, then had to stop.

"Wrong with you?" Dr. Wheeler finished. "I'm afraid I don't have the answer to that just yet. But we're working on it. So far we're leaning toward some kind of viral or bacterial infection."

"Can't . . . move too much . . ."

Dr. Wheeler looked surprised, and frowned. "Really?"

"Can't breathe . . ."

The doctor only nodded this time. "Try to get some rest," she said. "We'll talk again shortly."

Castillo said nothing. Instead, he thought of the frown on the doctor's face when he'd told her was having a hard time moving. Somehow, he didn't believe he and Dr. Wheeler would be talking again shortly.

If ever.

On Saturday morning, Frank Logan surprised his daughter by showing up at her door. It was unlike him, to say the least. Never mind that Jenna was mad at him, and that it was only nine-thirty, and she had no interest in getting up.

"Dad?" she rasped, leaning against the door and looking out at him. "What are you doing here?"

Frank smiled halfheartedly. "I guess that's the greeting I deserve for not calling first," he said. "I was uphill already, and though I'd come by and see if I could buy my daughter a late breakfast."

Jenna opened the door a little wider, though she was mindful of the fact that Yoshiko was still in the top bunk, trying to stay asleep.

"I'm not exactly presentable for breakfast," Jenna said with a forced smile of apology. "Not even a late one."

"How about an early lunch?" he asked. "I have time."

Barely able to suppress a sigh, Jenna shrugged. "I have a lot to do today. Getting ready for finals and all. If you'd called, maybe—"

"You would have had time to work out a better excuse?" Frank offered. "I would have called, Jenna. But you've been avoiding me all week. I'd like to talk to you. I know you feel like I'm abandoning you, or something, and I'm sorry for that. But I don't want you to take it out on Shayna, too."

He glanced around uncomfortably. "This isn't really the place for this, is it?"

"No," Jenna said bluntly. "Maybe you can write me from France?"

Frank flinched as if she had spit on him.

"I'm sorry." Jenna sighed. "That was harsh. Not that you don't deserve harsh, but maybe I don't have to be so childish about it."

"No," Frank said. "I'm sure you can be much more articulate in your attacks when you haven't been woken too early on a Saturday morning."

For a second, Jenna couldn't think of a thing to say. Then she just nodded. "I'll meet you downstairs in twenty minutes." She was tempted to add an apology, but didn't. She wanted him to earn it.

When she shut the door, she turned to find Yoshiko sitting up in bed looking at her curiously. Jenna sighed and shook her head, then pulled on her robe. She grabbed a towel and the wire basket she kept her toiletries in, and went to the door again.

"You're gonna crucify him, aren't you?" Yoshiko asked.

Her hand on the doorknob, Jenna paused and looked back at her roommate.

"I don't think so," she said, uncertain. "I don't really

want to be that selfish. But I want him to know his timing sucks."

Yoshiko smiled gently. "I think he knows."

It turned out that Yoshiko was right. Jenna and her father went to the Campus Center, the only place on campus to get something to eat at ten in the morning. Jenna sat across from him, eating yogurt and fresh fruit, and tried to get a handle on her anger. As childish as she knew it all was, she didn't find it easy to control those immature impulses. In fact, she wondered if she ever would.

For his part, Frank didn't bring it up right away. He asked how her mother was. Asked about her friends and her classes and her love life. She noticed that he studiously avoided asking if she'd had any second thoughts about her job with Dr. Slikowski.

Or maybe he figures it's over with, and doesn't see a need to ask about it. Which made her wonder why *she* kept thinking about it, if she was so sure it was over with. She was glad he didn't ask, though. She hadn't told anyone that her recent conversations with Slick and Danny had gotten her surfing the Net for similar incidents.

She didn't want to talk about that any more than she wanted to talk about the very thing they were supposed to be talking about.

Jenna wished she was still in bed, asleep.

"Mom lied to me," Jenna said abruptly.

Frank blinked a couple of times, and frowned. "How's that?"

"My whole life, she led me on about how I'd be a

grown-up someday. Like there was this magic switch that got thrown at some point, and suddenly, bam, adulthood. But it's a lie, isn't it? You all do it. Probably I will, too, one of these days. There's no such thing, is there?"

"I . . . guess I don't understand what you're getting at," her father replied.

"Sure you do," Jenna said. "I mean, I'm eighteen, and the whole grown-up thing? Nowhere in sight. But you're not really a grown-up either. Nobody ever really becomes a grown-up, do they? We get wiser. We learn more. We have more responsibility and that means we have to behave in certain ways, but the whole confident, mature, adult thing is pretty much an illusion, isn't it?"

Frank studied her for a few seconds. Jenna stared at him, searching his eyes. Finally, her father nodded slowly.

"Yeah. I guess it is. And you're right to be angry with me. I'm not going to lie, Jenna. The decisions that I made, about me and Shayna, and about the sabbatical, were made with very little consideration for you and how you might feel. I should have included you. I should have been more forthcoming and not just sprung it on you like that."

Jenna looked away. "I feel like whining that it isn't fair," she admitted, her voice soft. "But I really am happy for you guys. I just . . . I don't want you to go."

"I'm glad."

Taken aback, Jenna looked at him sharply.

"Not that it upsets you, but that you don't want me to go," he said. "I don't even know if I deserve that, but

I'm glad for it anyway. I love you, Jenna. I'm happy to be in your life, and I will miss you. But I'll be back in a few months and we'll just keep on. Plus there's e-mail, right?"

Jenna looked suspiciously at her father. "You're not exactly technowizard, Dad."

"I know how to use e-mail," he said defensively. "You know that. So I'm not much for the Internet. So far, I've managed to survive."

At that, Jenna fell silent. They ate the midmorning snacks that were passing as breakfast for them both in the relative quiet of the nearly empty Campus Center. At length she sighed and looked at her father, resolved to the inescapable fact of his forthcoming departure.

"You're a jerk," she said, half smiling.

"A truth your mother learned long ago," Frank agreed. Jenna chuckled at that.

"You don't hate me?" he asked hopefully.

"I don't hate you," Jenna allowed. "But don't think I'm not going to twist the guilt knife some more before you abandon me again."

"I can't ask the impossible," Frank said. "But, since you're talking to me again, there is something I wanted to ask you."

Jenna looked at him expectantly.

Frank grinned. "Shayna and I were wondering if you would be a bridesmaid."

With a laugh, Jenna nodded. "Okay. But if the dress is ugly, I reserve the right to jump ship."

"You've got it," Frank agreed.

*　　*　　*

Though it had been a bit warmer the past few days, Saturday afternoon brought a change in the weather. From seemingly nowhere, clouds rolled in and the sky became gray and dull. Though no precipitation seemed forthcoming, the temperature dropped more than fifteen degrees over the course of two hours.

In Sparrow 311, Jenna sat at her computer, surfing the Internet, searching for anything to help her make sense of the odd mystery that had presented itself to both the Boston and Somerset police departments. She'd had the window open a few inches most of the day, to get some fresh air, since she knew that winter was coming in and soon it would be nothing but super-heated air, clanking radiators, and stuffy rooms. About three o'clock, however, the climate change had her shivering at her desk, and she got up to shut the window.

With great longing, she stared for a few seconds at the poster of Hawaii that hung on the wall—it was home to Yoshiko, but Jenna had only ever dreamed of the place. Then she sat down at the computer again. She fiddled with a plastic brainteaser puzzle on her desk. It was shaped like a snake and she needed to work it around into the shape of a figure eight. She stared at the computer screen, at a loss as to how to proceed. After a moment, she decided not to bother. It wasn't her job, it wasn't her business, and she had finals to worry about.

Still, it really was a puzzle.

With a sigh, Jenna dropped the brainteaser onto the desk and moved the cursor over to shut down the computer. As she was about to do just that, the door opened and Yoshiko walked in, with Caitlyn Janssen and Olivia Adams behind her.

"Hey guys," Jenna said.

Her tone and her expression were pleasant enough, though things between her and Olivia had been a little awkward ever since Jenna and Damon had expressed an interest in one another.

Jenna thought it was ridiculous, but if Olivia didn't bring it up, she sure wasn't going to.

"Hey, J," Yoshiko said, smiling. "Please tell me you're doing research for finals, and not doing more zombie research."

"Zombies?" Caitlyn said, before Jenna could respond. "What bizarreness have you gotten yourself into now, Jenna?"

Jenna shot a nasty glare at Yoshiko, who only smiled in response.

"That's just Yoshiko being freaky," Jenna replied. "Zombies don't exist any more than vampires or werewolves do. Once you die, I mean really die, your brain cells start to rot right along with everything else. That's pretty much permanent."

"And thank you for the colorful image," Olivia said, face stretched into an expression of absolute disgust.

"So what is it, then?" Caitlyn asked.

She seemed genuinely interested, and Jenna was a little flattered. Yoshiko was a sort of partner in crime when Jenna got herself involved with these puzzles, there when her talents were needed, and interested in the outcome, of course. But Caitlyn's interest was different. She seemed to think Jenna's interest was, while very strange, also pretty cool.

It felt good.

"There've been a few crimes in the area lately, murders and robberies, that seem to have been committed by people who were supposedly dead and buried," Jenna explained, smiling self-consciously.

"That's impossible," Olivia said dismissively.

"Of course it is," Yoshiko said, looking at Olivia as though the other girl was a moron.

Which she wasn't. Jenna thought it odd, and wondered if Yoshiko was being extra defensive for her sake, because of the whole thing with Olivia and Damon. If so . . .

Good, Jenna thought. It wasn't the charitable way to feel, but Olivia didn't exactly make her feel very charitable.

"The problem is that most every reference I come up with that's at all similar either has to do with Christian resurrection, like Lazarus, or with zombies and voodoo and all that," Jenna said.

"Oh, here we go," Olivia said, laughing derisively. "So, what, the police are going to round up all the usual suspects, which in this case means Haitians, right?"

Jenna looked at her oddly. "Um, no. Actually, in this case, both of the guys who are supposed to have come back from the dead were Jewish. So, no real Haitian connection. And again, the voodoo thing is just what comes up on a Net search. I'm looking for something a little more concrete."

"So, what, then?" Caitlyn asked.

Yoshiko sat down on the broad windowsill. "Jenna's thinking hoax. Some kind of cover-up. They make a deal with the funeral home people, fake their deaths for insurance or whatever, then commit crimes they can't be prosecuted for 'cause they're dead."

Jenna shrugged. "Pretty much. Problem is, there's no real reason to think that. And the hospital records on both of the guys are pretty convincing. They were dead. Unless it wasn't them to begin with."

"How did you get a look at those?" Caitlyn asked. "I didn't think you were working at SMC anymore."

"She's not," Yoshiko replied. "And neither of them died at Somerset anyway. As for how she saw them, well, maybe she had some help."

"Oh, you bad little hacker, you," Jenna said, grinning at her roommate.

"I must be punished," Yoshiko admitted, hanging her head in mock shame.

"I don't get it, though. I mean, great and all, yea, Hardy Boys," Olivia said. "But if you're not working for the medical examiner anymore, why are you even bothering?"

Jenna looked at Yoshiko for assistance, but none was forthcoming. Yoshiko, in fact, looked like she'd like to have the answer to that question too. They weren't the only ones.

"Just curious, I guess," Jenna said, though she knew how lame that sounded.

"Me too," Caitlyn chimed in, looking at Olivia. "It's creepy, don't you think? I mean, don't you want to know what's going on?"

"I'm happy to read about it in the paper when it's all over," Olivia said. "I'm a little too worried about finals right now."

"Yeah, but not so worried that you're not going to the DTD party tonight," Yoshiko teased.

"Party?" Jenna asked. Then she looked at Yoshiko. "Are you guys going?"

Of course, she knew that Olivia and Caitlyn were going. They were both sorority sisters, and Delta Tau Delta was a decent fraternity. No way would they miss that party. By "you guys," Jenna meant Yoshiko and Hunter.

"Hunter said he'd go if you and Damon were going," Yoshiko replied.

Jenna didn't miss the look that Olivia shot her when Yoshiko mentioned Damon. As far as anyone else knew, they'd dated a few times. The fact that they were now sort of officially a "thing" was not known to the general public.

Obviously, that's about to change.

"I'll ask Damon," Jenna said. "If he's up for it, we'll definitely go. I could use some loud music and sweaty dancing."

"Ooh, now who's the bad girl?" Yoshiko said.

Jenna smiled, recognizing how much more confidence Yoshiko had gained in the few months they'd been at Somerset. She'd always had a lot going for her—smarts, humor, looks, perfect hair and a killer fashion sense—but when they'd first met, Yoshiko had been a little quieter, a little less willing to take the spotlight, even when it was offered to her. That had changed, and Jenna thought it was definitely for the better.

Yoshiko was her own woman now, no question. It made Jenna recall her earlier conversation with her father.

Maybe I jumped the gun, she thought. *Maybe there is something to this whole growing-up thing after all.*

"Well, then, sweaty dancing it is," Yoshiko said happily. "Maybe we'll even coerce you into playing Fuzzy Duck again."

"I hate that game!" Jenna said, laughing.

Then again, she thought. *Naaaaah.*

Dr. Wheeler looked down at Jason Castillo and chewed the end of her pen. "I just don't get it," she said. "I mean, it's like his whole system just collapsed."

Next to her stood Dr. Steven Jenese, a resident in emergency medicine who'd been in charge of the detective when he had first been admitted the night before.

"Weird," Dr. Jenese agreed.

"Weird doesn't even cover it. Pulmonary edema, uremia, hypothermia, paresthesia, cyanosis, never mind the obvious respiratory and digestive distress," Wheeler said, frustrated. "Makes me think of that fungal thing that killed Jim Henson."

"Who?" Dr. Jenese asked.

"The Muppets guy. The one who created them. Massive system failure. Not like here. That's not what I'm saying. Just that it came on so fast and so completely. It's almost like some kind of superallergic reaction or something."

"Maybe you're reading these charts differently, but all I see is a guy who had heart and respiratory deficiencies, probably from birth. They kick in now, slow oxygen to his brain, the whole body reacts, systemwide trauma. It happens."

"Like this?" Dr. Wheeler asked, looking at Jenese skeptically.

"I've seen stranger," he replied. "It's weird, but there's nothing suspicious about it. It's just too bad for the guy."

Then he pulled up the sheet to cover Jason Castillo's face. It wouldn't be long before an orderly came to wheel the corpse down to the morgue.

"I guess," Dr. Wheeler said. "It seems like a pretty scary way to die, though."

"If you think of a nice way, you let me know," Jenese told her.

chapter 5

In the squad room of Somerset P.D.'s homicide unit, Audrey Gaines stared at the documents in front of her and realized she'd read the same paragraph three times. With a sigh, she pushed back from the desk and stretched. It was gray and cold outside, and pretty much the same inside, the fluorescent lighting making the place look like a morgue. And Audrey should know. Her job gave her ample opportunity to spend time in morgues.

For a moment, she stared out the window, then turned back to her work, only to find her partner, Danny Mariano, watching her curiously.

"You all right?" he asked.

"Hardly. It's Saturday. I don't like working Saturdays. It's also a nasty day that I'd rather spend sitting in bed with a cup of home-ground coffee and an old Cary Grant movie on cable," Audrey said, then grumbled a moment. "This case is enough to make my ears bleed.

We've got nothing but a lot of information that doesn't match up, and some genuine impossibilities, and it all feels like a dead end to me."

Still frustrated, but satisfied with her rant, Audrey sipped from a cup of the awful sludge that passed for coffee in the squad room, and looked back down at the papers on her desk. They were the medical records and autopsy report for Adam Shefts, the dead guy who happened to be a suspect in the robbery-homicide at Pappas Jewelers.

"You like Cary Grant?" Danny asked suddenly.

Audrey frowned. "So?"

"Nothing." Danny shrugged. "Just figured you to go more for the Humphrey Bogart, Clint Eastwood, strong, silent types than the suave and charming types."

"Story of my life." Audrey sighed. "Yes, I like Cary Grant. Now, can we get on with Mission: Impossible here?"

Danny smiled. "It's grating on me, too, Audrey. The look on Shefts's mother's face is just . . . what do you say to her, you know?"

"I *don't* know, that's the problem," she confessed.

They had been to see Laura Shefts, the mother of their suspect-who-was-supposed-to-be-dead. She was a proud woman, early sixties, still grieving over the loss of her only son. Though Audrey and Danny had both been very careful with their words, it was impossible for them not to offend the woman. After all, they were suggesting that her son had not died at all, had somehow faked his death, and had now become a killer and a thief as well.

Mrs. Shefts had thrown them out.

Audrey figured they deserved it.

"If we could just get an order of exhumation," she began.

Danny cut her off. "Oh, sure. Feel free to ask the guy's mother about that. I'm sure she'll be happy to co-operate. Besides, we're pretty sure we know what we'll find, right? The Boston cops dug up that reporter's grave, found the remains of some John Doe down there. I expect there's another one in Shefts's grave."

"Maybe," Audrey replied. "But Boston P.D. had a corpse. They could prove their guy wasn't in his grave."

"And we've got fresh fingerprints," Danny snapped, leaning back in his chair and throwing his pen onto the top of his desk. "What do they think, someone cut off his hands before burying him, just to throw us off? That crap only happens in the movies."

He looked at her, awaiting a response. Audrey could only look back, a bit of nausea sweeping over her. "God, let's hope so," she said.

They stared at each other, and then, after a moment, both laughed in horror and disbelief and frustration.

It really is Mission: Impossible, Audrey thought. They had multiple witnesses who saw Shefts die, saw his corpse. He'd been identified after death by his own mother. She had held her dead son in her arms, despite the discouragement and discomfort of the morgue attendant.

Adam Shefts was dead.

Adam Shefts had recently committed a murder, weeks after his supposed death.

"You know what we're going to have to do, don't you?" Danny asked.

Audrey nodded regretfully. They'd been putting off trawling Shefts's old hangouts, mainly because the man was supposed to be dead, and if he arranged it to seem that way, he wouldn't be visiting his old hot spots. Not to mention that someone would have noticed. On the other hand, if he'd cared that much about being discovered, he wouldn't have stayed in the area.

And he would have worn gloves to kill Mrs. Pappas.

"Why didn't he?" Audrey asked aloud. "Wear gloves, I mean."

"Drugs," Danny suggested. "Our man was hopped up on the goofballs, or something. Or he thought the whole *dead* thing would protect him. Which it still might."

Audrey shook her head, growing angry now. "No, we'll find him. And when we do, we'll make him explain how he pulled this stunt off in the first place. I do think we should share information with the Boston P.D., though."

Danny smiled. "Mainly because they have more to go on than we do."

"Mainly, yeah," Audrey agreed.

She picked up the phone to call Jason Castillo.

Olivia and Caitlyn had made plans to have dinner downhill with some of their sorority sisters, which left Yoshiko and Jenna to their own devices.

"What time's the party?" Jenna asked.

Yoshiko looked thoughtful. "I think seven-thirty, but

I could be wrong. Why, you don't want dining-hall food? You love campus cuisine."

"Yes," Jenna agreed with mock seriousness. "But it is possible to have too much of a good thing."

"I don't know if I can handle pizza again tonight."

"How about Panda Garden?" Jenna suggested. "I'm sort of in the mood for Chinese."

Yoshiko thought about it a second, and then nodded. "I could do that. They do have the best Szechuan, and I'm feeling pretty spicy."

She said this last with a mischievous grin, but before Jenna could reply, there was a knock on the door.

"Who goes there?" she called, even as she went to open it.

"It's me," came the reply.

"Oh, well, *in that case,*" she teased as she pulled the door wide. She had recognized the voice, of course, but Hunter's tone had also held the suggestion that they should expect it to be him.

"So, what?" Jenna asked. "You think you're the only guy who comes by to visit us? 'Me.' What is that? It's like a revolving door around here, pal, so you'd better not start taking us for granted."

Hunter looked at Jenna for a long moment, and she tried to keep the mock-stern expression on her face as best she could. With a half smile on his face, he executed a deep bow.

"I beg your pardon, ma'am," he said, laying the Southern gentility on thick. "It was mighty presumptuous of me. I'm grateful that you suffer my presence so often."

"Now that's more like it," Jenna said. She glanced over her shoulder at Yoshiko. "What do you think?"

"He could use a little more work," Yoshiko said. "But I guess if you keep after him, at least we won't have to send him to charm school."

"Hey!" Hunter protested.

He swept past Jenna into the room, fingers pointed and at the ready as if they were weapons. And given how ticklish Yoshiko was, Jenna thought, maybe they really were. Hunter attacked, and Yoshiko giggled madly as she tried to escape the onslaught. Jenna rolled her eyes.

"All right, you two." She sighed. "Can we save the cutesy crap for when you're alone together?"

"Cutesy?" Yoshiko shrieked, still giggling, trying to catch her breath. "You think torture is cutesy?" She grabbed Hunter's hands, and turned him toward Jenna. "Punish her."

Hunter grinned as he looked at Jenna. He raised his hands, index fingers pointed at her.

"Oh, no," Jenna said. "Uh-uh. Down, boy. I'm not your girlfriend. I don't have to put up with that foolishness. Don't even—" Then she yelped as Hunter moved in on her, hands darting toward her sides, sneaking around to tickle behind her knees.

Jenna giggled. Just once. She couldn't help it. Then she shouted at him to cut it out, a broad grin on her face.

"Come near me again with those fingers and I'll kick you so hard you'll be neutered," she snarled.

Hunter stood up straight, threw up his hands, and

looked at Yoshiko. "A gentleman cannot argue with that logic."

Yoshiko glared at him. "Wimp." Then she grabbed her coat. "We're going to Panda Garden for dinner. Want to come?"

"I don't want to interrupt the female bonding," Hunter replied, raising his eyebrows suggestively.

"Uh-huh. You wish," Jenna sneered.

Hunter nodded in agreement. "I have sinned. Seriously, though, is Damon going?"

"He was going into town with Ant and Brick today. I'll leave him a message."

Hunter put his arm around Yoshiko. "I'm in," he said, and gave her a quick kiss.

"I thought you might be," Jenna said.

"Now who's taking who for granted?" Hunter asked.

Yoshiko tapped him. *"Whom."*

Hunter sighed. "I can't win."

"Nope," Jenna agreed.

She called Damon's room and left a message on his machine, letting him know where they'd be going for dinner, and asking if he wanted to go with her to the DTD party that night. Then she grabbed her coat, and they headed out.

It was a long walk off campus to Panda Garden, and it was colder than Jenna had expected. But she didn't mind the exercise, and she knew the hot food would taste even better because of it. Hunter had an arm around Yoshiko as they walked, and Jenna envied their warmth, so she stepped up on his other side, and Hunter put the other arm around her. They walked on like that for half a mile, and Jenna thought it felt nice. The three of them had been through a lot together, and yet, in some way, that simple moment together seemed perfect to her. She had never felt closer to them, her two best friends.

It also made her think about her best friends from home. Moira hadn't come back from USC for Thanksgiving. Priya, on the other hand, had been home, but very distant. Jenna had called her in the days leading up to Thanksgiving, and Priya had come by the Blakes' house on that night, but she hadn't stayed very long. Jenna knew Priya hadn't been having the best time in school, but that wasn't it. Things were getting better, or so Priya had told her.

It was more than that. Priya was at Northwestern University in Illinois. Moira was at USC for film school. They were growing up, and growing apart, and there was an awkwardness about Priya when Jenna saw her that only made that more obvious. All they really talked about was high school. The old days.

I didn't think I'd ever have old days, Jenna thought. She didn't like it.

Now, walking with Hunter and Yoshiko, as pleasurable as it was, she couldn't help but think about her friends from high school, and wonder if the love and intimacy she felt for her new friends would be any more durable.

Then, suddenly, Hunter and Yoshiko started to quicken their pace, and to skip, and they dragged Jenna right along with them.

"We're off to see the wizard," they sang, and Jenna joined them, just for a moment, until they all started laughing and slowed to a walk again.

Hunter hugged them both, and Jenna realized how crazy she was. *Just stop,* she chided herself. *Life goes on, that's what happens. Stop second-guessing everything.*

In that moment, she realized that continuing to look into this latest mystery was a mistake. That's what Slick and Danny and Audrey and all the rest of them were there for.

They don't call them the authorities *for nothing.*

With that decision, she felt a surge of relief, and she held on to Hunter a little tighter. There was a kind of freedom in the realization she'd had. For the first time since she had quit her job, she felt truly comfortable with that decision.

Which was when Hunter asked her the question.

"So how's the zombie hunt going?"

Yoshiko laughed. Jenna just gave a little shrug and let her arm drop from behind Hunter, stepping slightly away from him.

"Sorry," Hunter said. "Is that a bad subject?"

"No," Jenna said carefully. "Actually, I was just thinking about that. With finals and all, I think I'm going to leave the crime-solving to the people who get paid for it."

"Wow," Yoshiko said, glancing past Hunter at Jenna. "That's a total one-eighty. Don't tell me you finally found a puzzle that was too much for you?"

"No," Jenna said, and instantly regretted her defensive tone. She knew Yoshiko hadn't meant it as a challenge, but it put her on guard anyway. "But it's not my job anymore."

"And like you said," Hunter added, "you have finals to worry about. Not to mention a new boyfriend to occupy your time."

Jenna blushed at that one.

Yoshiko chuckled. "You know," she said, "Hunter believes in zombies."

"Get outta here," Jenna said, frowning at Hunter. "Tell me she's kidding."

Hunter seemed to mull that one over for a second. Then he glanced at Jenna. "You're Catholic, right?"

"Never went to church much, but I was raised Catholic, yeah."

"So's Yoshiko," Hunter said. "I'm a Baptist. Or at least my family is. Thing is, growing up in Louisiana, I met people, both adults and kids, who believe much more strongly in voodoo than the three of us put together believe in the religions we've grown up with. That doesn't necessarily include zombies, but for some people it does."

"Yeah," Jenna said, "but *you* don't believe in them. I mean, come on."

Hunter nodded once. "I believe that anything that inspires that much faith has to have a little bit of truth in it somewhere. I'm not saying the dead can come back to life—"

"They can't," Jenna interrupted curtly.

"No argument," Hunter replied. "But I figure there's got to be something to it."

Yoshiko tugged on his arm. "All I want to know is, do they eat brains?"

"I ever meet one, I'll ask him," Hunter replied. "Then I'll point the way to your room."

Jenna snickered. "Yeah, you're a prince."

Dr. Slikowski sat in his wheelchair in the morgue at Mass General hospital staring at the withered remains of the John Doe who had been exhumed from Marc Cohen's grave. Or, more precisely, what was supposed to be Marc Cohen's grave. He was not comfortable doing much more than a cursory examination here, and certainly would not attempt a full autopsy without an able assistant.

Not that he'd been asked to perform the autopsy. They'd asked him down out of courtesy only, since Alan Krupp, a pathology resident at the hospital who had once been one of Slick's students, had already informed him of the circumstances of the Cohen case. No, if they'd wanted his help in the autopsy, they'd be in the autopsy room now, instead of the morgue.

And the dead man would have been prepared for an autopsy. He hadn't. In fact, the rotting clothes, moldy with the smell of the grave, still clung to the remains.

Slick might have asked to do an autopsy, if he thought he'd have the proper assistance. This whole thing was baffling, and he wanted to know more. He found himself wishing that Al Dyson had accompanied him.

Back at Somerset Medical Center, the autopsy room was specially equipped for him to be able to work from his chair. Though he was frequently called to consult and to perform autopsies at other hospitals in the county, he was never comfortable doing so because he was forced to rely on others for much of the work.

Slick hated to rely on anyone else to do work that was his responsibility.

"From what you've told me, I presume the *actual* remains of Mr. Cohen are also here in the morgue?" he asked.

Chet Fredericks, the chief of pathology at Mass General, cleared his throat. "The police asked us to hold Mr. Cohen's remains for now. Certainly, there is no doubt that his death occurred just as the police report indicates. Though we did find some poison in his system, it doesn't seem to have been responsible for his behavior, or his death."

Slick glanced back at Fredericks. "Poison?"

"Datura," Fredericks elaborated.

"That's damned peculiar." Dr. Slikowski narrowed his eyes and studied the corpse before him as best he could considering his vantage point. "You agree it's reasonable to expect, from a visual examination of the unidentified DOA, that the autopsy will reveal the time of death to be roughly current with the false report of Mr. Cohen's *first* death?"

"Correct."

The M.E. studied the skull of the corpse. "Cause of death will likely prove to be massive cranial trauma."

"So it would seem."

"Do the police have any clue as to his identity?" Slick asked.

"Not yet," Fredericks admitted. "They're assuming some relation to Cohen, but not ruling out a random murder in order to fill the coffin. I'm told they're checking missing persons reports from the time of burial."

Slick sniffed. "They needn't bother. No one's likely to have reported this man missing. He was almost certainly single and homeless."

Fredericks sniffed. His tone, when he spoke, was doubtful. "What makes you say that, Doctor?"

The tone was what did it. Slick was done there. He'd spent enough time with Chet Fredericks. He pushed back his wheelchair, forcing Fredericks to step out of the way, and began propelling himself toward the door of the autopsy room. Just before he reached it, he turned to look at the other doctor.

"There's no wedding ring on the corpse," he said. "Whoever killed this man probably wasn't interested in robbing him, so it seems likely he wasn't married. As for his being homeless, take a look at his shoes."

Fredericks did. Slick didn't have to. Even from where he sat now, near the exit, he could see what he'd spotted the moment he'd entered the room. The dead man's shoes were worn and scuffed, the heel eroded, and the soles had several holes in them. No one who had a choice would have worn those shoes.

Someone murdered a homeless man to make sure there was a corpse in Marc Cohen's coffin during the funeral, and when it was lowered into the ground. It seemed likely the murderer was Cohen himself. He'd certainly proven himself capable of that act. But none of that explained the recent murder of Lois Pappas, at which the murder weapon proved to be covered with the fingerprints of yet another man who was supposed to be dead.

"Curiouser and curiouser," Slick whispered as he wheeled himself down the hall to the elevator.

Then, just as he'd wished for the company of Al Dyson earlier, he found himself wishing Jenna were with him. He would have liked to hear her opinion on all of this.

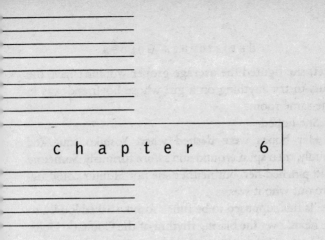

c h a p t e r   6

Melody had hated fraternity parties. Jenna remembered so clearly the Arts House party they'd gone to, where they'd danced for hours. Damon had kind of blown her off that night, months earlier, and Melody had told her how nasty she thought frat parties were. Drunken slobs and smoke-filled rooms, music too loud, guys groping any woman who passed; Jenna had laughed at the description then.

She wasn't laughing now.

If Melody was still alive, we wouldn't even be here, Jenna thought. It wasn't quite as bad as Melody had described the parties she'd been to, but neither was the description entirely inaccurate.

Drunken slobs, check. Loud music, check. Smoke, check.

The groping was really the only thing missing from the list, and Jenna thought that might have more to do with the fact that she was very obviously with Damon. From her admittedly limited experience with the subject, she figured the average groper wouldn't have the guts to try anything on a girl whose boyfriend was in the same room.

She hoped.

Her hopes were dashed when Yoshiko squeaked loudly, then spun around and swore furiously. Someone had pinched her, but neither she nor Hunter could figure out who it was.

"Is this supposed to be fun?" Yoshiko asked loudly, to be heard over the blaring rhythm of the Goo-Goo Dolls.

"I guess I thought it would be more like the party at AOPi last month," Jenna said, and shrugged. "That was pretty crazy, but nothing compared to this."

They all agreed. The party at AOPi sorority had been much more controlled, much more social. People had been there, in Jenna's estimation, to have a good time together, to meet people. To have a party, in other words.

This isn't a party, she thought, looking around. *This is an NFL locker room.*

In the corner where the keg sat in an ice-filled barrel, a hulking guy sprayed beer from the tap directly into the mouth of his beer-drenched buddy. Not far from that spectacle, a girl erupted into a fit of giggles as three stumbling guys broke into a chant demanding that she lift her shirt and show them her breasts. Jenna had already had to navigate around vomit once so far, and she didn't look forward to having to do it again.

Granted, not everyone behaved that way. Most of the fraternity brothers and their guests were laid-back, having a good time, drinking beer and joking or flirting, even dancing in one of the front rooms, where there was *almost* enough room to move. She'd seen a couple of guys she knew tangentially from her biology class, both of them DTD brothers, and they seemed civilized enough.

But with the smoke and the music and those who seemed unable to stop themselves from behaving like animals, Jenna thought it felt more like a crude circus than a party.

"Hey," Damon said into her ear, just loud enough to hear. "I'm going to hit the bathroom. When I come back, we can take off if you want."

Jenna looked up at him and smiled gratefully as he slipped off through the crowd. It closed behind him, crushing her and Hunter and Yoshiko together at the center of the herd.

"Hey, when Damon comes back, you guys want to leave?" she asked.

"I thought you'd never ask," Hunter said, relieved.

But Yoshiko didn't seem to be relieved. Jenna thought she looked more torn than anything.

"We haven't even seen Caitlyn or Olivia," Yoshiko said. "I told them we'd be here."

"Could be they've already been and gone," Jenna suggested.

"If they're smart," Hunter added. "The two of them walking in here without dates'd be like throwing the Christians to the lions. You should see the basement. It's a pit. There's an inch of beer on the floor down there."

The three of them started to laugh, but their amusement was abruptly cut short when Hunter was shoved roughly from behind. He turned around angrily and found himself face-to-face with Brian Duffy, a broad-shouldered musclehead with a bad attitude and a serious drunk-on. Duffy was in Jenna's American lit class, but he barely even glanced at her as he bore down on Hunter and poked him in the chest.

"Hey!" Hunter snapped.

"Hey yourself, loser," Duffy sneered. "If you're having such a bad time, why the hell you even still here? You must be a moron, standing in the middle of the house bad-mouthing the place."

Hunter wasn't a big guy. He stood maybe five ten, and though he wasn't bony or anything, he was pretty thin. Jenna tensed, wondering how he would respond, and almost stepped in herself to tell Duffy to back off. But Hunter didn't give her the chance. His right hand flashed up and he slapped Duffy's jabbing finger away.

"Thank you," Hunter said, smiling. "You've proven my point. And thanks also for the suggestion." He turned to look at Yoshiko. "Let's get out of here."

For his part, Duffy looked astonished. But Jenna saw it for what it was: an act. Anyone who was paying attention would have seen that he was the kind of guy who relished that sort of thing. He wasn't stunned by Hunter's reaction, he was thrilled by it.

"Don't walk away from me," Duffy snarled, and shoved Hunter from behind. "You turn your back again, I'll break your neck."

Hunter lunged for Duffy, but Yoshiko held him back, whispering something to him sharply, though Jenna couldn't make out the words. Duffy laughed, beckoning to Hunter to try it again.

"Back off, Brian," Jenna snapped at him.

Duffy glared at her, then seemed to recognize her. "I know you, don't I? Babe, you've got bad taste in friends, you come in here with a guy shootin' off his mouth, raggin' on DTD."

"Yeah, truth hurts," Jenna sniffed. "Go back to your cave. We're leaving now. You can continue the floor show without us."

Jenna turned and grabbed Hunter's arm, spinning him around and, together with Yoshiko, propelling him toward the exit. She knew that if Damon came back looking for them, he'd realize they'd gone outside to wait.

But Duffy wasn't giving up that easily.

"You're a sassy little bitch, aren't you?" Duffy sneered. He grabbed Jenna by the hair and yanked her back, then ducked down and sniffed at her like he was a dog. "I like that. What? You think being a girl means you can mouth off and there aren't any repercussions?"

Jenna gritted her teeth to stop herself from crying out, though the pain in her scalp was awful. She reached up and grabbed at his hand, then she tried to kick him. Part of her—the part that could detach itself from the pain—knew that Hunter was about to try to come to her rescue, and get his ass kicked as a result. It was inevitable, and it was just what Duffy—*the bastard*—wanted to happen.

Then, suddenly, Duffy grunted in pain and let go of her hair. Jenna spun around to see Damon hauling *him* backward by the hair. He got his foot behind Duffy and sent him sprawling to the floor, where he knocked against a pair of girls who had been watching his intoxicated performance entranced.

"You think being a big, drunken moron means you can act like a total asshole and nobody's going to call you on it?" Damon said, echoing Duffy's own question from a moment before. He held up both hands, dismissing the fallen drunk. "Well you're wrong. There's nothing wrong with this fraternity that getting rid of embarrassing freaks like you wouldn't fix."

With a roar of fury, Duffy tore himself up off the floor and lunged at Damon. Hunter slipped past Jenna and Yoshiko, ready to fight, no matter what. But Damon wasn't planning to fight. Duffy threw a stumbling punch, and Damon whipped up a hand and knocked it away, sending the drunken idiot plowing into another group of partygoers.

A crowd had started to gather, but no one tried to stop the fight that seemed destined to happen.

Duffy glared at Damon. "This is none of your business—"

He clenched his jaws, cutting off the rest of the sentence. But Jenna thought she knew what it was going to be. A word that would have changed everything. It wouldn't have been just a fight, then. Drunk as he was, Jenna was surprised Duffy bothered to hold back the racial epithet she knew was on the tip of his tongue.

"You grab my girlfriend like that, it becomes my business," Damon said softly, and yet somehow Jenna could hear every word over the music. "Hell, even if she wasn't my girlfriend. I've got no respect for a guy who'd stand by and watch your little circus act without stepping in."

All along, Jenna had thought Duffy looked drunk and cruel, but now his expression changed. It became vicious. But before he could try anything more, someone shouted off to the left, and Jenna looked to see four DTD brothers pushing through the gathered crowd. She recognized one of them as Ed Switzer, who had been an acquaintance of Melody's. The others were all new faces.

"What the hell's going on here?" asked the one in front, a square-jawed, well-dressed guy Jenna liked right away.

"These jerks were sayin' all kinds of nasty stuff about the frat, man," Duffy sniffed, glowering at Damon. "Girl got all up in my face, and then her boyfriend here tried startin' a fight."

The one Jenna liked glanced over at them, his eyes stopping on Damon.

"Hey, D," he said, a half smile on his face. "You causin' trouble in my house?"

"It's my way, Vic," Damon replied. "You know me."

The guy, Vic, shook his head in disgust as he glanced back at Duffy. "Brian, sometimes I'd rather spend a week with a bunch of pledges than have you in this house another night. Go sober up, or find somewhere else to sleep it off."

Vic looked at the other DTD brothers around him. "Duff's cut off for tonight. Anyone sees him drinking, tell me." He stared hard at Duffy. "One more thing like this, man, and you're gone. Got it?"

Duffy swore, turned, and staggered off toward the stairs.

"You enjoy yourself, all right?" Vic said, turning his attention to Jenna and her friends. "See ya later, D."

"How the hell do you know him?" Hunter asked as Vic and the other DTD brothers merged back into the herd.

"He's in my drama class," Damon replied.

Jenna shook her head in wonder at that, but didn't comment. Instead, she glanced over at Hunter and Yoshiko, who were whispering to one another. "So," she said. "Time to go?"

"Past time, I'd say," Yoshiko replied.

Damon put his arm around Jenna, and the four of them started for the door. They hadn't gone a dozen feet when someone screamed behind them. Jenna spun around, and darted her head from side to side, trying to see through the crowd.

"Now what?" Damon said, almost to himself.

In the midst of the crowd, Jenna saw Ed Switzer stand up and glance around anxiously. He shouted for Vic, and then Jenna saw Vic himself pushing through the partiers.

Jenna found herself moving forward, almost without thinking about it. Damon spoke her name, but she kept on, slipping in front of people, moving through the group. Something bad had happened, and she wanted to help. She was curious, of course, but her time working with the police and the M.E. had given her a weird sense of responsibility that she hadn't really even recognized in herself until now.

"What happened?" she asked a girl in front of her.

"No idea," the girl said. "He looked real sick, shaky and all, and then he just fell down right there." She nodded down.

Down, at the still form of a pale guy with blond-dyed hair and a tattoo on his biceps. He lay sprawled on the floor, no sign of any injury. But Jenna noticed instantly that he wasn't breathing.

"Tim!" Vic shouted at the kid on the floor. He slapped Tim's face. "Hey, Parish, get up!"

"Move!" Jenna snapped, and shoved past the other people in the way. Vic glanced up at her as she slid to her knees beside him. "Do you know CPR?" she demanded.

"No," Vic said. "I . . . what do you . . . ."

Jenna ignored him. She'd learned CPR in high school, but she'd never had to use it before. Now she started pumping on Tim Parish's chest for all she was worth, tuning out the mutterings around her. Minutes passed. She sensed Damon at her side, and was glad he was there, but she didn't dare stop. She didn't dare.

Until she heard the ambulance siren, and she realized how long she'd been trying to revive the poor, sickly-looking kid who lay there on the beer-sticky floor.

Above her, Vic leaned in to look down at the still form of Tim Parish, who seemed so young, Jenna was sure he must have been a freshman pledge.

"Is he dead?" Vic asked.

Jenna just looked at him. To his credit, she thought Vic looked more concerned about the kid's welfare than about the storm of trouble on the horizon, once it got out that the kid had died on the premises.

Then Damon helped her up, they joined Hunter and Yoshiko, and the four of them went out to wait on the front steps for the EMTs to come in. The police would come, too, Jenna knew, and they'd want to talk to everyone who'd been in any way involved.

It was going to be a long night, but Jenna didn't really mind. She was thinking about Tim Parish, wondering how he died. Wondering why he died. And she was thinking about his family, for whom the answers to those questions would mean so very much.

That night, at five minutes before eleven o'clock, Adam Shefts walked into Lafford Square Liquors in Somerset with a .38 Special in his hand and ordered the clerk to open the register. Once the register was opened, Shefts shot the clerk, in full view of the security camera. He emptied all five bullets from the Smith and Wesson revolver into the clerk's chest, with no expression on his face whatsoever.

He left the store with more than eleven hundred dollars in cash. Up until that point, it had been a very good night.

The sky was clear on Sunday morning. Despite the cold, Jenna and Yoshiko had left the window open just a crack, and Jenna was already awake when she heard the distant bells of Sacred Hearts church chime seven o'clock. Though her mind felt a bit fuzzy, and her eyes burned a little because she was still so tired, she could not force herself back to sleep.

Torture, she thought. Sunday morning, and she could sleep as late as she liked, but here it was, seven o'clock, and her mind was racing. *No more sleep this morning. And little enough last night.*

Every time she closed her eyes, she saw the party again. The people, crowding around. Ed Switzer, shouting for Vic, the anxious expression on his face. Yet somehow, she couldn't see Tim Parish's face in her dreams. When she woke, she realized that she couldn't even remember what the dead boy had looked like.

That haunted her worse than her dreams. More than anything, it was that which kept her from falling back to sleep.

I ought to at least remember what he looked like. But all she could recall was the feeling of his cold, unmoving chest beneath her hands as she tried desperately to get him to breathe.

By seven-thirty, she had accepted the hard truth that the sandman was not coming back for her. Jenna was on her own to face the day. With a sigh, she dragged herself out of bed and pulled on her sweats, then zipped her black leather jacket all the way up to her chin. She needed air. She needed out.

For some reason, she didn't want to be there when Yoshiko woke up. If she stayed, she knew she'd have to talk about the night before, and how she felt about it, and she didn't think she'd be able to put that into words. Not just yet.

So she walked. It was early enough that there weren't very many people out and about, except for runners and bicyclists, enjoying their morning constitutional. Jenna waved to a few of them, but she also made certain that she kept her walk to open areas. It wasn't that she really feared some kind of attack. Who could live with that kind of paranoia 24/7? But she had also made it a point, ever since what happened to Melody, to try not to go alone into any place that was particularly isolated.

There was no real direction to her stroll. No destination. Her feet took her across both uphill quads, then past the chapel and down the stairs by the library. She walked up Sterling Lane, but turned back up the hill long before she would have passed DTD. That was someplace she didn't want to go this morning.

The walk exhilirated her, helped to clear the fog from her mind. As she started across the grass toward the front door of Sparrow Hall, she realized that the time to think—or to simply let her thoughts drift—had had another effect on her. It had crystallized her feelings about a great many things.

The night before, a stranger had died at her feet. His name had been Tim Parish, and he was a freshman, just as she was. From things she'd heard afterward, as the police questioned the partygoers, Jenna knew he was from Framingham, which was right next to Natick, the town where she herself had grown up. Though they'd never met, it chilled her to know that it might have been her, there on the floor of the frat house, beer staining her clothes.

Contemplating those things had also made her think about Tim Parish's mother and father. There would be an uproar, of course. The media would splash it everywhere. Even if Tim's death had been completely natural, it would be spun to seem as though he'd died from alcohol poisoning, and another rash of fraternity hazing stories would run on the local news. It was sort of a fall ritual.

But none of that would give anyone even the remotest hint of the grief Tim Parish's parents would go through.

Jenna had tried to save Tim. She'd failed at that. But she knew that there was a way she could still help, a way she could make it just a tiny bit easier on Tim's parents.

When she returned to her dorm room, Yoshiko had gone out to breakfast and left her a note. Jenna was happy to have the room to herself. She went down the hall and took a long shower, then pulled on comfortable, worn black jeans and an olive turtleneck, soft and warm. She needed that at the moment.

Then she picked up the phone.

"Hello?" The voice was tinged with the rasp of sleep, and she cringed to think she might have woken him. But she wasn't about to back out now. She'd seen, more clearly than ever, what she was meant to be doing.

"Dyson, it's me. Jenna."

"Hey," he said, suddenly much more awake. "What's wrong?"

"Nothing," she said, though a bit too quickly. Her

tone revealed a lot, she knew, but she didn't have the energy to hide it. "Listen, are you free for lunch later?"

"You okay?" he asked, still prodding, worried for her.

"I will be," she assured him.

"Hang on," Dyson said.

Jenna heard him speaking to someone in a muffled whisper, as if he had covered the phone, and she felt embarrassed. A moment later, he came back.

"What time?"

"Um, noonish? Listen, I'm sorry if I interrupted anything. I guess I wasn't really thinking, and—"

"Jenna, come on," Dyson chided her. "It's just Doug. He stays here half the time because he's too lazy to clean his own place. Hey, if he plays his cards right, you may find *him* answering the phone pretty soon."

"I'm glad it's going so well," Jenna said sincerely.

"Now let's not get carried away," Dyson said doubtfully. "The guy doesn't know a damn thing about sports. Which means I may have to kill him. Anyway, noon is fine. Where?"

"Up to you," she said.

"Well, considering you're without real transportation, and I have to drop by the office anyway, do you want to meet there? Then we can drive anywhere you want to go."

"That sounds great," Jenna said happily. "And, hey, if you want to bring Doug—"

"You kidding? He'll probably still be sleeping when I get back."

*   *   *

"Are you sure about this?" Dyson asked, gazing at Jenna intently.

"Very."

He leaned back in his chair. Slowly, his grave expression gave way to one of delight. Dyson shook his head and laughed, then jumped up out of his chair and went to wrap his arms around Jenna, where she sat on the edge of the desk.

"Jenna, that's the best news I've had in a long time," he told her. "The caring friend in me, y'know, with the whole big-brother complex, is still worried about you. But the rest of me, which is admittedly pretty selfish, is thrilled to have you back. And I know Slick will be too."

"You really think so? He seemed pretty disappointed in me before," she said anxiously.

"He'll be ecstatic, are you kidding? He'll have his protégée back."

Jenna blushed a little at that. She had told Dyson about the death of Tim Parish, and how seeing him die had made her realize that quitting in the first place was a mistake. Not that she wanted to put herself in danger again anytime soon, but she couldn't stay away from the puzzles and the mysteries of their job. She wanted to give people the answers that would help them sleep at night.

She had just wanted to tell Dyson about it before she talked to Slick.

"Do you want me to tell him?" Dyson asked, looking at her as though he understood her anxiety perfectly.

"No," she said immediately. "I'll come in tomorrow, and I'll talk to him then. I'd really like to be there for Tim Parish's autopsy."

"That'll be two tomorrow," Dyson said. "We also have a Boston cop, Jason Castillo. He's down in the morgue. He died at Lawrence Memorial, but it was apparently a weird one. He was also the Boston P.D.'s detective on the Marc Cohen case. You know, with the—"

"I know it."

"Well, they've asked Slick to do the autopsy."

"Why didn't he just do it there?" Jenna asked.

Dyson shrugged. "They're not even ten minutes from here, and you know how much easier it is for him to work in his own space."

Jenna knew immediately what Dyson was referring to. Somerset Medical Center's autopsy room had special features designed to make it easier for Slick to work from his wheelchair. Of course it would be easier for Slick to do an autopsy there. And if the other hospital was so close, there was no reason not to do it.

"I'm in," Jenna said. "I'm also hungry. You ready?"

"Actually, I just have to run down to the basement. I left a tape in the autopsy room on Friday, and I wanted to drop it off for transcription tomorrow morning on my way in. We've been using a professional transcriptionist since you abandoned us."

Jenna pouted at his teasing, and Dyson grinned.

"Anyway, I'll meet you in the lobby."

But when they rode the elevator down, Jenna went all the way to the basement with Dyson. There didn't seem to be any reason for her to wait in the lobby, and she didn't want him to get the impression that she was skittish about the autopsy room. Not when she had just given him her whole speech about how this job was her purpose in life, and all that.

So when the elevator doors opened on the basement, they stepped off together. Their soles slapped the linoleum floor, and beneath the fluorescent lights, they both looked as though they belonged on a slab in the morgue themselves.

It was creepy for Jenna, with so few people around. But it was also nostalgic, in an odd kind of way. She missed working with Slick and Dyson, and she missed the excitement and fascination of participating in autopsies, delving into the puzzle of how a person had died.

She was still contemplating these feelings when Dyson slowed his pace. Jenna glanced at him and saw a look of alarm on his face.

"What?" she asked.

Dyson only pointed. A short way down the corridor was the door to the morgue attendant's tiny, lightless office. The door was slightly open, and someone lay on the ground, half in and half out of the office. Silently, they moved closer, but Jenna didn't recognize him.

"Who is it?" she whispered.

"Alex Panza. Morgue attendant," he replied, also in a whisper.

Jenna was about to crouch to examine the unconscious man further when they both heard a voice coming down the hall, rising in pitch and intensity. It was a kind of song, a chant.

A ritual.

Not fifteen feet from where they stood was the door

to the morgue. It stood open four or five inches. There was light in there, and the voice came from within.

The chant stopped. The voice continued. "Hear my voice," it said. "Obey me. Rise and walk, now, into a new life as my servant. Can you hear my voice?"

Then, cold and numb and completely without emotion, a second voice responded.

"I hear," it said. "I obey."

chapter 7

"Go," Dyson whispered. "Call the police."

Jenna glanced quickly at him and frowned. They had looked into the morgue attendant's office and found that his phone line had been torn out of the wall. There were phones in the morgue and autopsy room, of course, but that was very much in the wrong direction. She was about to argue that they should both get the hell out of there, but then she realized that one of them should try to get a look at whoever was in the morgue to describe them to the police.

She didn't even want to think about the exchange she'd just heard coming from inside the morgue. Or the chanting. It all sounded a little bit too much like someone was being raised from the dead, like a zombie. No way was she even going to entertain that possibility. But she felt a chill run through her just the same as she thought of the creepy, croaking voice she'd heard only seconds before.

"Jenna," Dyson urged.

The door to the morgue was only a few yards away, and it hung open several inches. They had no way of knowing how long it would be before someone came out, but they couldn't take chances. Jenna nodded to Dyson and gestured for him to move back farther into the small office of the morgue attendant, to be out of sight should the intruders emerge. The attendant himself was unconscious on the floor.

Dyson waved her away. "Go," he whispered.

Jenna turned to go, moving down the corridor toward the elevator as fast as she could while trying to remain quiet. She'd only managed to get about twenty feet when she heard the sound of metal slamming against metal, and she knew that she hadn't been fast enough.

Slowing, she turned to see two men emerging from the morgue. Neither of them looked good. She didn't want to acknowledge the thought, but she couldn't escape the idea that both of them looked too pale, sickly, even dead. The real difference between the two was that one of them wore nothing but sweatpants and untied sneakers and a winter coat, and didn't seem to have anything else on. No socks, no shirt. Nothing.

"No way," Jenna whispered, as she tried to force away the word that ricocheted around her head. *Zombie.*

The one who was fully dressed, the one she assumed had been chanting the rituals, spotted her. He didn't shout and break into a sprint to attack her. Instead, he slowly pointed in her general direction.

"Girl," he intoned. "Come here."

"I don't think so," Jenna snapped, walking backward, unable to tear her eyes away from them.

They were awful. Though one had apparently come to the morgue to retrieve the other, both seemed like hollow shells of men, shambling, barely coherent creatures with malignant intent.

"Girl!" the clothed one said again, this time with a little more emphasis, yet still not yelling. Then he turned to the other, the one with no shirt beneath his winter coat. "Kill her," he said, without any expression at all.

The zombies, if that was what they were, started after Jenna, quickening their pace. She could easily have outrun them, though. And she would have, if Dyson hadn't chosen that moment to lurch out into the corridor in front of them.

"Jenna, run!" he shouted.

The one who had spoken reached out, quicker than Jenna would have expected, and grabbed Dyson by the throat. With both hands, he started to crush Dyson's windpipe.

Jenna screamed as loud as she could. And not only once. She screamed again and again and she ran at them. The shirtless, silent man moved toward her, but he seemed sluggish and slow, almost like a sleepwalker. Jenna slapped his hands away from her and then hit him in the face with all her might. His lip split, but only a few drops of blood came out. He staggered back, and Jenna lunged out and grabbed for the arm of the one choking Dyson.

"Leave him alone!" she roared.

Dyson fought it, no question. He beat at the man's

face, tried to punch and kick the zombie, but he was already running out of air.

Taking a deep breath, Jenna screamed some more, not in fear, but alarm, praying that someone would come to their aid. It was Sunday at lunch time, and there couldn't be very many people around, but she hoped that some of the administrative offices down there would be occupied. Anyone.

Anyone, she thought.

"Hey!" a voice echoed through the basement corridor. "What the hell's going on down here?"

The pale, emotionless man released his grip and Dyson slumped to the ground. The shirtless one had gotten up, and the two of them moved for the emergency stairs. They slammed through the door, setting off an alarm. Jenna looked to see an orderly she recognized, Tony Xin, running down the hall toward her. Tony had been the one to yell, to scare them off.

"Tony, call security!" she shouted, then turned and ran to Dyson. Jenna held her breath as she knelt by him. When she saw him stir, she finally exhaled.

"Al," she gasped. "Are you okay?"

Dyson looked at her as though she were insane. "Sure. Fine," he said, rubbing his head as he sat up. "Why wouldn't I be?"

Sunday night, Jenna and Damon sat on the floor of her dorm room, pillows propped up against her bunk, and watched television without really paying attention to what was on. Jenna sat in front of Damon and lay back against his chest, his arms curled around her. She felt good and safe and warm there, but it didn't stop her mind from going back to the basement of Somerset Medical Center earlier in the day.

"I mean, broad daylight, you know," she said. "They ran right out through the emergency room. By the time the orderly called security, they were in a car and tearing out of the lot. I was there for an hour after that, and the police hadn't been able to find them in that time. It's just so freaky."

"No argument from me," Damon said, leaning his chin on her shoulder and holding her even more tightly. "I'm just glad you're safe. Couple of lunatics break into the morgue for some weird ritual, who knows what they'll do?"

Jenna stiffened slightly, and Damon obviously felt it.

"J?"

"Only one guy broke in," she said. "Dyson and I both identified him from police photos. His name is Adam Shefts. He was supposed to have died six weeks ago."

For a second, Damon said nothing. Then, very deliberately, he slid out from behind Jenna and moved around so he sat facing her, holding her hands.

"You know that's impossible, right?"

Jenna gazed at him, heart heavy with dismay. "The other guy, Damon? His name was Jason Castillo. He was a Boston cop, working this whole case. He died a couple days ago. Dr. Slikowski was supposed to do his autopsy tomorrow." She felt tears welling up in her eyes and forced them back, biting her lip. "I saw him, Damon. Walking around, very much alive. I heard them talking in the morgue. I heard . . ."

Her words trailed off and she looked away, mind reeling. She hadn't really allowed herself to think about it much that day, and now that they were speaking of it, all of her horror and fear and wonder began to overwhelm her.

"Jenna," Damon said softly. He took her hands and lifted them up, and kissed them softly.

Reluctantly, she looked up and gazed into his eyes. He was so serious, so emphatic, that she was entranced by that gaze.

"You know it's impossible," he told her. "You do. It's got to be some kind of hoax, some scam to cover up for the crimes they're committing. You know there's no—"

"There's no such thing as zombies," Jenna said, distraught. "Of course I know that. But I also know what I saw with my own eyes, and until I find the truth of it, that's going to haunt me. If it had happened after dark, I don't even know if I'd be able to sleep tonight."

Damon blinked, and stared at her in surprise.

"What?" Jenna asked. "Look, I'm not saying I think it's possible. I mean, it's probably drugs or something, they've got some kind of huge scam going, just like you said. But if you'd been there, Damon, God, the whole thing was just so eerie, and they looked so—"

"That's not it," Damon interrupted, a half smile on his face. "You're not a fool, Jenna. I'm sure you've already starting figuring out ten possible angles here."

"Then what?" she asked, concerned.

"You said until *you* find the truth," he reminded her. "Which I take means you, personally. You're going to get your old job back, aren't you?"

Jenna took a deep breath. Then she nodded. "I have to, D. Between that poor kid last night, and now this? I know most people would just let it slip right past them to the people who are supposed to be responsible for all this, but I don't have it in me. I can't just let it go, or it really *will* haunt me. These people all have families who need answers, the cops need answers, and I need the answers, too."

She said this last in a defensive tone, waiting for an argument, fully expecting Damon to try to talk her out of it. When she and Damon had first begun the long series of flirtations that would lead to them becoming a couple, they had run into one another at a party, where she had told him about the new job she had taken. He had been obviously appalled by it and had excused himself, and she hadn't seen him again that night. Since then, he had seemed far more open-minded about it, even respectful, but there had been no hiding that he was glad she didn't work for Slick anymore.

Truth be told, Jenna didn't blame him. Damon was creeped out by the idea of her spending her afternoons holding human organs in her hands. That was the reaction most people had.

But that night, Damon surprised her. He took a long breath and then pulled her close to him. He held her tight, and when he spoke, it was more like a whisper in her ear.

"I get afraid for you." His breath was warm on her neck, and his fingers twined in her hair. "It's supposed to be just a lab job. A nasty one, all right, but that's all. But you push and you push and you make it your business to see things through to the end. That's one of the things I admire most about you, Jenna. You're so damned brassy and you don't even see it. But it makes me want to hold you close, just like this. You're like a trouble magnet, all this stuff you get into. *I get afraid for you.*"

Jenna closed her eyes, relishing the feeling of his arms around her and his lips on her neck as he kissed her there.

"Good," she whispered.

Then Damon lifted his gaze and stared into her eyes. Though Jenna smiled, his expression remained serious, even when his lips met hers and they kissed deeply, his fingers in her hair and her hands running over his back.

It was a long kiss, and they both kept their eyes open. At least, at first.

On Monday morning at nine-thirty, Danny walked up the granite steps in front of the building that housed the Somerset P.D., sipping from a cup of Dunkin' Donuts coffee. Though the sky was perfectly blue, and the sun glared powerfully down upon him and the winter coat he wore, Danny shivered slightly.

It was a cold one, promising winter all too soon. He could see his breath, merging with the steam that rose from the hole he'd torn in the lid of his coffee cup. He took another sip, and savored the strong blend.

Inside, he greeted several people, and received the usual Monday morning reaction: *Glad to see you but I wish I was home.* With a minimum of socializing, he went up the stairs to the room on the second floor where the members of Somerset's homicide unit spent way too much of their time. He expected Audrey and Lieutenant Gonci to be there already, but Danny was surprised to find the squad room filled when he entered.

Audrey cast him an admonishing glance, and Danny quickly looked at his watch.

"I'm sorry, am I late?" he asked, scanning the faces of the cops gathered there, and stopping, eventually, on Lieutenant Gonci's weathered, rugged features.

"Actually, Danny, you're right on time," the lieutenant said. "It just turned out that everyone else was here early."

"We want to get moving on this thing, Detective," added an older, dark-haired woman whose hair was pulled back in a severe braid.

"Of course," he replied, nodding to the woman. Danny didn't recognize her, but he knew most of the other police officers gathered in the room. "I'm sorry to keep you all waiting."

Under most circumstances, such an apology would have garnered at least one "not at all," or some other, similar comment. Not today. The subject at hand was too much on all of their minds, and Danny knew that. He slipped his coat onto the back of his chair, then walked around to lean against the front of the desk, his coffee cup still in his hands. The others had already moved the other chairs in the office into a rough circle that effectively blocked anyone from walking through from the door of the squad room into the lieutenant's office.

Not that it mattered. Nobody was going anywhere just yet.

"I suppose I ought to make the introductions," Lieutenant Gonci said reluctantly. "My people on this case are Detectives Audrey Gaines and Danny Mariano."

Audrey and Danny nodded to those gathered around the circle.

"Tara Lizzotte, Medford P.D.," the lieutenant went on, gesturing toward the woman who'd spoken when Danny first entered. She raised a hand tentatively, and then dropped it.

"I expect you all know Detective Sergeant Flannery, Cambridge P.D.?"

Joe Flannery offered a halfhearted wave and grimace that reminded Danny of Archie Bunker. But then, Flannery almost always reminded him of Archie Bunker.

Gonci went on to introduce Marty Krelnick and Tricia Farano—a pair of Boston detectives Danny had met once before—and their lieutenant, Hal Boggs, whose clothes Danny thought looked so well pressed and creased it was a wonder they didn't cut him to ribbons when he put them on.

"So what the hell do we know?" Boggs asked when the intros were done. "I got Castillo's family breathing down my neck, never mind the press, the mayor, and the commissioner."

"We're all in the same situation, Hal," Lieutenant Gonci said. Then he glanced around, his eyes settling on Audrey. "Who wants to start?"

Audrey stood up straight and gazed at the gathered police officers. "I think we've gotta put one thing on the table right now. Whatever's going on here, we're not dealing with dead people. If that means we've got to stretch the truth with the press, then I think we've got to do that. We can't let the local press start running stories about zombies, or we'll all look like idiots."

"Well, clearly it's a hoax," sniffed Tara Lizzotte. "But it's a very elaborate one. I'm not even sure how involved Medford P.D. ought to be, considering that, obviously, Detective Castillo isn't dead, which means he did not die in Medford."

"That's going to sound just great in the press, Detective," Lieutenant Boggs scoffed. "But if you want to play it that way—"

"Hal," Gonci warned. "Can we stick to the purpose of this meeting?"

Boggs glared at him, but nodded slightly.

"All right," Audrey continued. "So far, we have three people whose deaths have been faked. Marc Cohen, Adam Shefts, and Jason Castillo. Without Castillo in the mix, we had a picture developing. Cohen and Shefts were both Orthodox Jews, which meant no embalming. Both of them were buried out of the same funeral home.

"Between Castillo's written reports, the exhumation of Cohen's grave, and Walter Slikowski's observations about the corpse found there, it's clear that someone replaced Cohen by murdering a homeless person and dumping the corpse in Cohen's coffin."

"Before burial, or did they dig him up after?" asked one of the Boston detectives.

"We don't know, but I don't know how much that matters," Danny put in. "Point is, murder was committed to cover up the hoax."

Audrey went on. "Since the Shefts family won't let us do an exhumation to check and see if anyone's buried *there,* we can't be certain the same pattern was repeated. But we can be sure it isn't Adam Shefts, since he left his prints behind at the robbery-homicide at Pappas Jewelers. Not to mention that we have two eyewitnesses identifying him yesterday at the hospital, and video from the holdup Saturday night.

"So Cohen and Shefts fake their deaths to commit theft and murder without getting caught," Audrey continued.

"But they do it very badly," Danny added.

Boggs chuckled. "No doubt there. But what about Castillo, now? He was on duty when Cohen killed those dealers. He was there when they shot Cohen to death, for Christ's sake. Cohen tried to kill him. It doesn't sound like these guys were in this thing together."

Tricia Farano, one of the Boston detectives, cleared her throat. "Jace Castillo is not a wrong cop. I don't care what he's done. Which, so far, isn't very much. Maybe someone's got something over him. Doesn't matter. Nobody's gonna convince me Castillo's turned."

"I've met him a few times," Danny said. "Castillo always seemed on the up-and-up to me. He was on the job 24/7. I hope you're right, Trish. But we've got him with Adam Shefts yesterday. His death was a fake. Unlike the others, he was scheduled to be autopsied, and he would've been embalmed even if there wasn't an autopsy. They had to get him out of there. Point is, he's still alive. What else are we supposed to make of that than Castillo's in this thing up to his eyeballs?"

Farano stared at Danny for a long moment, and then she looked away.

"All right, does anyone have anything to add here?" Lieutenant Gonci asked. When no one responded, he continued. "Medford, Boston, Cambridge, and Somerset have agreed to cooperate on this. So has Watertown, though so far they're only connected by the burial sites. That means searches and a statewide all-points for Shefts and Castillo. So far, charges against Castillo are minimal. Let's hope it stays that way. Way I see it, we won't really understand what's going on here until we can talk to one of these men."

"I'm with you on that," Lieutenant Boggs noted. "But we've got squat to go on so far. The car Shefts was driving yesterday was stolen. Other than beating the bushes and talking to relatives and known associates, we're just spinnin' our wheels. It'd be nice to know how the hell they're pulling this whole thing off."

"Any kind of lead would be helpful at this point," Farano added.

"Lieutenant Boggs is right, though," Audrey said. "The how of it is key, here. That's why we've got Walter Slikowski working on the case. All the research that entails is funneling through him. Mass General and Lawrence Memorial are both cooperating with us on that. He's the County M.E., so we didn't have any arguments there."

Gonci glanced around the room. "Let's get to it,

then," he said. "Before the *Herald* starts running front-page stories about zombies."

In the bright sanctuary of his office, Slick stared down at the medical reports on his desk and frowned. The sultry voice of Cassandra Wilson rose like smoke from the speakers on the bookshelf that stood against the far wall, but it brought him no comfort, no relief from the stress that had been building since the night before, when he'd received a call from Al Dyson.

The medical records on the deaths of Marc Cohen and Adam Shefts were embarrassingly slim. On the other hand, the doctor who had been treating Jason Castillo at the time of his supposed death had been quite thorough. Slick had even talked to her on the phone. The infuriating part of it all, the part that embarrassed him, though he would never speak of it to anyone, not even Dyson, was this: according to those records, Jason Castillo was dead.

But if that were the case, Dyson would not have seen him walk out of the morgue the previous afternoon. He was obviously not available for tests, to find the origin of this miraculous turn of events, and neither could such tests be made from blood taken during his illness. The records of the tests that had been run at the time were certainly still available, but they were nowhere near enough to answer Slick's questions. Worse yet, the autopsy on Marc Cohen hadn't produced any information that was helpful to them at all.

Or did it?

Slick wheeled himself out from behind his desk and over to the filing cabinet where he kept folders on any case he still considered active. It was a simple matter to pull the file on Cohen. All of the path lab results were in there. And Slick found what he was looking for.

Datura. It was a poison, though since Cohen was shot to death it had nothing to do with his demise.

So what was he doing with Datura in his system?

It wasn't much, particularly when he had no way to see if the other two men had the substance in their systems as well. But it was a start.

Dyson appeared in the doorway, interrupting his thoughts with a quick knock.

"Walter, you have a visitor," Dyson explained.

Slick raised an eyebrow at the grin on Dyson's face. But then the other doctor stood aside, and Jenna Blake walked into his office. Despite the smile on her face, she seemed uncomfortable, even a bit nervous.

"Jenna!" Slick said happily, propelling his chair toward her. "What a nice surprise. I was just thinking about you a little while ago. Are you just paying us a social visit, or have you finally realized the error of your ways and come back to join us again?"

When he saw Jenna flinch, Slick felt immediately guilty. "I'm sorry, Jenna," he said. "I was only teasing you. It's nice to see you, as always. What can I do for you?"

With a shy smile, Jenna met his gaze. "Well, you can give me my old job back."

Slick leaned back in his chair and stared at her in astonishment. He took his wire-rimmed glasses off and laid them on his lap.

"Miss Blake," he said, smiling, "that is the best news I've had in weeks."

chapter 8

Before heading to Nadel Dining Hall for lunch, Jenna went back to Sparrow Hall. In her room, she called and left her father a message on his machine. Then she called her mother, hoping to get her machine as well. To her dismay, April Blake answered the phone on the second ring.

"Mom?"

"Jenna. What is it?"

"Just surprised to get you, that's all. I was just going to leave a message."

April laughed. "If you want, I can hang up and you can call back and talk to my machine."

Sounds good to me, Jenna thought. But she kept that thought to herself. As a surgeon, her mother had odd hours, but that didn't usually mean she'd be home at noontime on Monday.

"Everything all right, Mom?" Jenna asked.

"The usual," April replied. "I'm just taking a little breather. I lost a patient this morning."

Ah. That's it. Her mother frequently needed some downtime if one of her patients had died on the operating table. It had always been the most difficult part of the job for April, and her mother's reaction to those losses had been a part of her own fear of becoming a surgeon, and holding someone's life in her hands.

"Sorry to hear that," Jenna said. "Maybe I should call you back later?"

"No, no, what is it, honey? I'm fine, really. What's happening with you?"

So Jenna told her.

At first, April said nothing. Then she only sighed. At length, she cleared her throat, and said the last thing Jenna expected.

"Good for you, Jenna."

"What?"

"Good for you," April repeated. "I worry about you. Always. I'm your mom, it's the job. But I can't always be there to protect you. The best protection you've got is your own intelligence and good sense. You walked away from this thing, turned it all over in your head, and realized that it really is what you wanted.

"It terrifies me, but I have to respect that decision. Just, please, try to leave the real investigation to the people who get paid for it, all right?"

Jenna was stunned. Her mother had opposed her working for the medical examiner from the very first time that she had been put in harm's way. It was weird, but part of her was terribly disappointed to receive her mother's blessing on it. Knowing that her mom was there as a safety net had always been a comfort to Jenna, even when it meant arguments and sulking.

Now the safety net was gone.

"I don't know what to say," Jenna confessed.

"Now there's a novelty," April teased.

"Hey!" Jenna protested. But only halfheartedly. She and April had always been friends, in addition to being daughter and mother. As an only child without a father around, she'd spent an awful lot of time as one-half of a dynamic duo. That had given Jenna a lot of opportunity to have input into her own life without actually growing up.

This was different. It was just what she'd wanted, of course, to be allowed to grow up, to make her own decisions, to be recognized as an adult. But it was a little frightening, too.

"I love you, Mom," Jenna said. "Thanks. You don't know how much it means for you to say that."

"What, like you'd even listen to me?" April scoffed.

"You'd be surprised," Jenna said.

"When do you start back?"

"Today. I went in this morning and talked to the M.E."

"Well, not wasting any time, are you?" her mother said. "But then, you never do. Tell Walter Slikowski he'd damn well better look out for my little girl."

Jenna grinned and shook her head. "I'll tell him exactly that, Mom."

Thirty seconds after she hung up the phone, it rang. Jenna zipped her book bag—notebooks and International Relations texts safely ensconced within—and went to answer it.

"Hello?"

"Hey. It's Danny."

"Hi," Jenna said, a bit surprised to hear from him. "What's up?"

"I just heard you were back on the team."

"Word travels fast," she marveled. "Or, at least, it does when Dyson's in the loop. What a gossip."

"Actually, we heard it from Slick," Danny corrected her. "He seems really happy you've changed your mind. We'll all be glad to have you back, Jenna."

"Except Audrey," she noted.

"Well, yeah, there's that," Danny admitted, and she heard the amusement in his voice. "But you can't ask for miracles. They just happen."

There was a pause. Uncertain what to say, Jenna checked the clock on Yoshiko's desk and realized she wouldn't have time to eat if she didn't hurry.

"Look, I've got to jet. I appreciate the call. I guess I'll see you later."

"Actually, that was what I wanted to call about," Danny explained.

"How so?"

"I guess I just wanted to make sure things weren't going to be weird between us now," he said.

Whoa, Jenna thought. *Now I get it.* Danny hadn't really called to tell her how glad he was she was coming back. In fact, it sounded like he might not be glad at all. Though he'd had as much of a crush on Jenna as she'd had on him—at least, that was what he'd told her—he'd made it clear that he could never be involved with someone her age because of the damage that might do to his rep, and the flak he'd catch from his co-workers.

Now he wanted to make certain there'd be no strain between them on the job because of their previous infatuation.

Jenna wanted to punch him.

Fortunately, the urge only lasted a few seconds. Forced to confront her own feelings on the subject, she realized that she really couldn't fault him for it. It was a reasonable question, and a logical concern.

"We're good, Danny," she said. "Don't worry about it. I'm looking forward to seeing you again. I mean, we're friends, aren't we?"

"Well, yeah," he said, though tentatively.

"Besides," Jenna added, "I *have* a boyfriend."

Adam knew exactly what he had to do. There was very little else he knew for sure. When he tried to think beyond it, to remember the past or question what he was doing, things just got all fuzzy. It was wrong. Stealing from people.

Killing. He had killed, he remembered that. That was terrible. Evil. But also necessary. It had to be done. He wasn't supposed to let anyone stop him, no matter what. If that meant killing, well, that was all right. *Whatever it takes.* The words reverberated in his mind. *Whatever it takes.*

He stood leaning against the brick wall of the T station in Lafford Square, watching the doors of the building across the street. That was where he had to go. He knew that.

Whatever it takes.

Eyes wide, rarely blinking, body mostly numb, Adam stepped off the curb and started across the street. A car screeched to a halt, barely avoiding hitting him, but Adam didn't flinch. He walked to the opposite curb and up to the glass and steel doors of the Somerset Savings Bank.

He swung the door open and stepped inside. Two seconds later, he passed through a metal detector, and an alarm sounded. The security guard was standing seven feet away, and he turned to look at Adam with the bored expression of a man who'd heard Peter cry wolf way too many times. The metal detector was too sensitive and went off over the dumbest things sometimes. The last one had been a fishing weight a young guy had on his key chain.

Adam shot the security guard in the center of that bored expression, destroying his nose and showering the carpet and desk and the frumpy female loan officer behind him with blood and brain tissue and fragments of the guard's skull.

The body fell back onto the desk and then slid off, and the things that had sprayed from inside the man's head smeared on the oak and then started to soak into the carpet.

There was a lot of screaming. It was a distraction for Adam and it made his head hurt. It made him worry that he was going to get in trouble for this. But then he reminded himself that the only thing that would get him in trouble was not bringing back the goods.

Bring back the goods. Those were orders. *Whatever it takes*.

The jewelry store and all of that stuff had been fine, but eventually Adam realized what he had to do. To keep out of trouble. He didn't want to get into trouble. The bank. That was the best idea yet. If he brought back the goods from the bank, then he might even get what he really wanted.

He might even learn his last name.

It bothered Adam that he couldn't remember his last name.

But not as much as the screaming. The last name was something that'd come in time. The screaming, though. He could do something about that.

So he shot the frumpy loan officer in the throat and she fell down, gagging, trying to scream some more, bleeding and crying at the same time. Then he waved the gun around with his right hand.

His left hand moved up to his mouth; he put a finger to his lips.

"Sssshhhh," he whispered. "Quiet."

He didn't know if they could hear him over the alarm from the metal detector, but it didn't matter. They got the point. They stopped screaming. Adam walked over to the tellers and raised the gun again. He pointed its muzzle at a pretty red-headed girl behind the counter. Something stirred in him as he looked at her. Something nice.

Adam smiled at her.

"Oh, God, please don't . . ." the pretty girl with the lush red hair whimpered and started to cry. "Just hold on and I'll give it to you."

She started to put money in a cloth bag. Adam smiled even more broadly. He would have liked to kiss the girl, but that would have meant lowering the gun.

Out of the corner of his eye, he saw someone move. Without letting his right hand waver at all, Adam reached into the rear waistband of his pants, beneath his jacket, and pulled out a second gun. He glanced over, saw the muscular, middle-aged man who had been about to leap at him now frozen in fear.

Adam shot him in the chest.

The redheaded girl leaned over on the counter, sobbing, barely able to hold herself up. Adam frowned. Poor girl. He put the second gun back into his waistband, reached over the divider separating them, and grabbed the bag, which was now full. Then he moved along to the next teller, and aimed the gun at her head. This one had dark, dark hair, cut short. She looked angry.

Adam didn't like her.

But she was quickly shoving money into a bag for him, so he let her live. He didn't want to shoot anyone if he didn't have to. That wasn't why he had come here.

While the third teller was filling a bag, Adam heard a strange whimper behind him. It sounded almost . . . excited. He turned to see where it had come from, wondering if he was going to have to shoot anyone else.

There were three police officers in heavy black vests standing inside the doors of the bank with their weapons drawn. They had snuck into the building while his back was turned, which wasn't exactly fair, in his book. All of the people in the bank had moved aside, crawling out of the line of fire. The tellers dove on the ground behind the counter.

"Drop the gun right now!" one of the cops screamed at him.

It hurt Adam's head.

He turned the gun toward them, but he didn't move fast enough. All three opened fire on him. Bullets tore through his chest and his arm, and Adam's gun flew from his hand as he fell to the ground, bleeding. His entire body was numb, except where the bullets had struck him.

Those places were blazing with pain, burning.

Adam felt them, and he was very glad that he could.

Whatever it takes, he thought, and with his left hand, the one that still worked, he reached back and pulled out his second gun. He shot one of the cops in the chest before they killed him.

When Adam died, bleeding out all over the floor of the bank, he still couldn't remember his last name.

It was the smell of formaldehyde that did it. Jenna had shown up at Slick's office right after her International Relations class to find the M.E. and Dyson waiting for her. She had asked that they let her participate in the autopsy on Tim Parish, and Slick had agreed. So when she walked through the door, the two of them were at Dyson's desk, glancing over some documents together. But, really, they were just waiting for her.

Together, the three of them had ridden the elevator down to the basement. Upon stepping off, they were bathed in that eerie fluorescent lighting, and Jenna stole a nervous glance at Dyson. Judging by his pallor, she thought he might be a bit anxious as well. They'd been down there the previous afternoon, and shared perhaps the strangest experience of their lives. The memory of that experience distracted Jenna as they walked down the hall toward the autopsy room.

Once there, Slick used his key to open the door, and the three of them went in together. Jenna glanced around the room, immediately filled with a sense of familiarity. The room was loaded with gleaming metal equipment, from the scales to the overhead camera to the countertops and the large metal autopsy table with its huge vent above. A microphone hung next to the vent.

It was all so familiar to her that Jenna felt almost as though she had dreamed the intervening time, that she'd never really stopped coming here. It had been less than a month—not so very long at all—but it was almost surreal how little time it felt had passed.

It was the smell of formaldehyde that destroyed that illusion. It was an acid stink that began, immediately, to burn her nostrils and make her eyes water. She blinked and pinched her nose.

"Are you all right, Jenna?" Slick asked, brow furrowed with concern for her.

Dyson chuckled. "She's fine, Walter. It's just been a while since she's been down here, right, Jenna? The formaldehyde getting to you?"

Slowly nodding, Jenna smiled sheepishly. "I'd gotten used to it. But I guess I've been gone long enough that—"

"The cells inside your nostrils have grown back," Dyson interrupted. "That'll teach you to quit on us. You're like Al Pacino in the *Godfather* movies."

Jenna laughed with him. "Just when I thought I was out, they pull me back in," she groaned, quoting Pacino.

"Al," Slick said, all business. "Why don't you retrieve the subject from the morgue?"

"On it, Dr. Slikowski," Dyson replied, his own formality including a bit of teasing.

Then he slipped back out the door they'd come through, leaving Jenna and Slick alone for the first time since she'd decided to return. He sat in his wheelchair and removed some of the stainless steel instruments they'd need from the metal drawers on the far side of the room. When he was through, he took off his glasses and used his shirt to wipe the lenses. Without being asked, Jenna went to the lockers and retrieved lab coats, caps, and masks for both of them. She handed a set to Slick, and he took them with a thin smile.

"I'd forgotten all about the smell," he told her. "I remember the first time you came down here, and how much it bothered you. I suppose I've been down here too long, eh?"

"Who knows?" Jenna replied, slipping into her coat. "Maybe the formaldehyde fumes alone are preserving you? How to stop the aging process: eat one apple and do two autopsies every day."

There was a tone in her voice that even Jenna didn't

recognize until Slick glanced up at her oddly. He studied her a moment, apparently trying, just as Jenna was, to decide exactly what was in that tone.

"Are you all right?" the M.E. asked. "Perhaps you shouldn't have started today, so soon after that episode yesterday."

For some reason, Jenna thought of her father then. There was an irony here that made her sad. Frank Logan had left her mother when Jenna was young, and though he had made an effort toward paternal expressions of love and support since she'd arrived at Somerset in September, now he was going away again. How Jenna felt was not one of her father's priorities, and never had been.

It was twisted for her to think this way, for she knew that it wasn't really true. But part of her thought Slick cared more for her feelings than her own father did, and that bothered her profoundly.

"I'll be all right," she said, smiling wanly. "It's just, well, I was there on Saturday night when Tim Parish died. I tried to do CPR, actually."

"Oh, my. You should have told me that," Slick protested. "I'm not sure you should—"

"It's one of the reasons I came back," she interrupted. "I didn't know him, if that's what you were thinking. Never met him before. But when he died, all I could think about were the people who would be waiting for the results of his autopsy, needing to know, all of that."

There was more she might have said, and she knew it. But Jenna stopped then. Slick stared at her a long moment, then let out a deep breath. He nodded.

"All right," he said. Then he softened somewhat, and allowed a small smile. "Welcome back."

Before Jenna could reply, there was a rap at the door. She opened it, and Dyson was there with Tim Parish's cold body on a gurney. A tag with his name and file number hung from his toe. As always, there were no clothes on the corpse. It had never really registered with Jenna before. After death, the human body was no longer a person to her, but a thing, an object. But for some reason, her memory of trying to save him on Saturday night made her slightly embarrassed to be seeing him unclothed, even though he was dead.

She pulled her mask up to cover her face, hiding the fact that she was blushing slightly. Then she helped Dyson wrangle the body up onto the autopsy table. Slick moved his wheelchair into place and locked down its brakes. Then he thumbed the lever that lowered the steel table and tilted it down toward him slightly.

"Scalpel," he said, his voice a bit muffled through the mask.

Jenna snatched a scalpel from the steel countertop and placed it into Dr. Slikowski's outstretched hand. Slick clicked on the tape recorder using the remote control unit, and Jenna glanced up at the microphone above them.

"Subject, Timothy Parish; autopsy 619-337-21," he began. "Caucasian male. Age eighteen. Height, five feet eleven inches; weight, two hundred and twelve pounds. Visual examination reveals contusions, probably received when subject collapsed. Tattoo on left shoulder of Greek comedy and tragedy masks. Faded surgical scar on right knee. No other external markings. Rigor is severe, but an odd lack of settling of the blood is noted."

Jenna watched as Slick brought the scalpel up and placed its tip where he always did, at the center of the chest, over the breastbone. Her mind went back to the party two nights earlier, and her efforts to save Tim Parish. More than ever, she wanted to find out what had killed him. She was glad to be back on the job. Jenna knew she had made the right decision.

Slick pressed the tip of the scalpel down and the skin dimpled for a moment, then split. The instrument was very sharp. The M.E. dragged the blade carefully along the center of the dead kid's chest. Three inches. Four.

There was blood.

Then Tim Parish opened his eyes wide, and began to scream.

chapter 9

The dead kid's scream echoed off the gleaming steel of the autopsy room, and Jenna stared at him in mute horror. She felt not paralyzed but wholly numb. As though she herself was the unmoving corpse.

Of course, this corpse was far from unmoving. As Dr. Slikowski had begun the autopsy, and cut into his chest, Tim Parish had opened his eyes and screamed.

After that, it was just chaos.

"My God!" Slick shouted.

Tim's hand gripped the M.E.'s wrist, shoving the scalpel away from him. Slick pushed away from the autopsy table, his wheelchair rolling back to crash into the steel counter and drawers.

"How could this happen?" Dyson cried out, sounding frenzied. "Walter, how the hell—"

"I don't know!" Slick snapped. "Just get him up to the E.R. Now! Move it!"

Dyson did move it. He went to the autopsy table and

tried calming Tim down, even as he began to edge him over.

"Jenna, get the gurney and help me!" Dyson said.

But she was frozen. Slick wheeled himself to the phone and punched in numbers, then started barking instructions to whomever answered on the other end—someone at the E.R., she assumed.

"Jenna!" Dyson called again.

But she couldn't respond. The kid was screaming still, almost unintelligibly. There was fear and pain in his eyes. He didn't try to get up, but he looked around the room, even as his wound spilled blood over his skin. His gaze locked on Jenna, and that was what snapped her back to reality.

With a quick stride, she went to the gurney and slid it over next to the autopsy table. She slipped her arms beneath Tim's legs as Dyson lifted his upper body, and together, they moved him to the gurney. Then they were speeding for the door.

"They're waiting for you!" Slick shouted. "Go, go! And, Al! Get a complete breakdown of everything in his system. Blood work, cell samples, everything."

By that time, they were already rushing down toward the elevator with Tim Parish on the gurney—no longer screaming but now hyperventilating and staring around wildly—and Slick had rolled into the hall to call his instructions after them.

"How is this possible?" Jenna asked Dyson, mind whirling as so many questions flew by faster than the corridor around them.

Dyson looked at her nervously, then down at the kid on the gurney. "It isn't," he said. "It really isn't."

Jenna didn't argue. *What good would it do?* Instead she ran ahead to punch the button for the elevator. When Dyson pushed the gurney up behind her, she turned and leaned over the panicked boy.

"Tim," she said, her voice even. "You're going to be all right. We're taking you up to the E.R. right now."

"What . . ." he croaked, voice raw from screaming and weak from lack of use. "What . . . happened?"

Jenna glanced quickly at Dyson, who frowned at her.

"We'll find out," she promised.

It was only in the elevator on the way up to the E.R. on the first floor that she had time to be amazed at herself. Jenna hated to see people bleed, hated the idea of someone's life in her hands. That had been one of the reasons she had gravitated toward pathology in the first place. Murder scenes horrified her, but it wasn't the same. The dead held no real terror for her.

The dying, on the other hand . . .

But Tim Parish wasn't dying. Quite the opposite, in fact, he had seemingly come back to life. In all the chaos and the shock of it, with the urgent need to get him to the E.R., where they had the tools to treat him—tools unavailable in the autopsy room—the blood had not bothered her as she would have expected it to.

She wondered if that meant she was over her fear, or simply too overwhelmed to think about it.

"I . . . know you . . ." Tim croaked, where he lay on the gurney.

Jenna only looked at him oddly. It was possible, she supposed, that Tim had seen her on campus, or even that he was in her bio class, which was large enough that she might not have noticed him. But he sounded more sure of himself than that.

"It's all right, Tim," she said, confused. "It'll be all right."

They were hollow words whose truth she had no confidence in, but they were all she had.

"I know . . . you . . ." he said again. "You were there. Gave me . . . CPR. Tried to . . . save me."

Jenna's eyes widened. She turned to look at Dyson, who didn't seem to be listening. Tim was right, of course.

When he'd died, there on the floor at the DTD party, she had tried to save him. Even that wasn't exactly right. It was possible he'd remember her if she was trying to save him. But she hadn't been. She had been trying to *bring him back.*

He was already dead. He couldn't possibly . . . she thought. Then she cut off that train of thought, because he lay there before her, a testament to the impossible.

"We'll talk later," she said. "After they've fixed you up. I'm Jenna."

"Jenna," Tim repeated.

The elevator doors opened, and Jenna and Dyson rushed him headlong toward the E.R. Orderlies appeared ahead of them, clearing the way. Several people who had strayed from the lobby area stared as they went by.

Other doctors were there suddenly. An E.R. surgeon and a couple of nurses.

The surgeon stared at Tim in horror, then looked up at Dyson. "How in God's name—"

"No idea," Dyson snapped. "But that's for later."

"All right," the surgeon replied. "We'll get him stitched up and go over his vitals."

"Dr. Slikowski will be up shortly," Dyson said, keeping pace with them as they moved Tim into a room where they could work on him. "He'd like a complete blood and cell sample workup."

The surgeon raised his eyebrows without looking up—all his concentration was on Tim now. "Yeah," he said. "This is gonna make one hell of a story." Then he glanced up at the two nurses sharply, and over at Jenna and Dyson. "Let's not share this with the media, please. At least not until we know what really happened here."

Jenna and Dyson agreed, and then were politely ushered from the room by one of the nurses. Out in the corridor, they walked slowly back down the hall toward the elevator. When they reached it, Jenna went to punch the button. Dyson stopped her.

"Slick'll be up in a minute. Let's just wait for him."

She nodded, and they stood silently together until it became uncomfortable. At length, she glanced up at him.

"You know what I'm thinking about," she said.

Dyson wouldn't meet her gaze, but he nodded. "Yesterday."

"Yesterday," Jenna echoed.

"It's impossible, Jenna. You know that."

"I used to. But we just saw it, Al. With our own eyes."

"It's impossible," he insisted. "There's some other explanation. A scientific one."

But he still wouldn't look at her.

*　　*　　*

As far as Danny Mariano was concerned, funeral homes smelled a little too much like hospitals. On most hospital wards—with the telling exception of maternity—he'd always found an underlying odor of decay. Of death, or impending death. Cancer and ICU wards were the worst. Over that smell there was always a weird combination of antiseptic and perfume that was worse, in some ways, than the formaldehyde smell of an autopsy room. That was a clinical, chemical smell. The smell of science. It wasn't trying to *hide* something.

Which wasn't to say that funeral homes necessarily had that smell of decay. But that combination of antiseptic and perfume, and worse, in a way, the additional smells of flowers and powder—or the pancake makeup they used to give corpses that especially terrifying wax-museum look—disturbed him. Distracted him.

All of which contributed to the fact that while Audrey was interviewing David Greenspan, the director of the Katz Funeral Home in Watertown, Danny was trying very hard to concentrate on the conversation, and failing. He didn't want to be there. But he wasn't about to bail on Audrey, either. With the death and apparent resurrection of Jason Castillo, and the *second* death of Adam Shefts, their case had heated up about a thousand percent. Nobody knew what the hell was going on, but they had to find out.

It wasn't going well. As if they didn't have enough cops on the case, the Watertown P.D. were now taking an active role. Everyone was playing relatively well together, considering how small the sandbox was, but that wasn't likely to last very long. The pressure to figure out exactly what the hell was going on was already becoming almost too much to bear. Pressure came right on down from the governor to the mayors of the cities involved to the police commissioners to the captains to the lieutenants, building up mass and momentum until it landed squarely on the shoulders of the detectives who were actually supposed to do the work with all that pressure on them.

It was not a good day. And the way Danny figured it, the forecast for the rest of the week looked just as bad.

First thing that morning, Watertown P.D. had interviewed the grave diggers and security personnel at the cemetery where both Shefts and Cohen had supposedly been buried, and had come up with nothing. Boston P.D. were looking into Castillo's private life, but Danny had to wonder if they'd share anything incriminating they might find. Castillo was one of their own, after all. Medford P.D. were cooperating, but that consisted of little more than access to crime scenes, and helping to search for Adam Shefts. Same thing with Cambridge.

"Nobody's looking at the big picture," Danny had said to Audrey after their meeting broke up that morning.

"So let's look," Audrey replied.

Which led them here. Danny wished he'd kept his mouth shut. Audrey had already established with Greenspan that Shefts and Cohen hadn't been embalmed. They'd known that from Castillo's notes already. Greenspan himself seemed edgy, but Danny didn't blame him. The whole thing was freaky, and Greenspan's reaction seemed normal. He was a pretty good judge of people. Had to be, on the job. He didn't think Greenspan was anything more than what he seemed to be.

"How did Detective Castillo seem to you when you spoke to him?" Audrey asked.

Greenspan frowned. "I'm not sure I take your meaning."

"Was he just going through the motions, did you think, or was he really digging?" Danny elaborated.

"Trust me," Greenspan said dryly. "He was digging. I had the feeling he thought I was involved somehow. I suppose that would be a natural assumption. But that isn't the case." He said that last part quite emphatically.

"We're not suggesting it is," Audrey assured him.

"I saw those men buried. I prepared their bodies for burial. The facts of this case seem . . . unimaginable to me." Greenspan looked at the perfect carpet. He shifted on the perfect, mutely floral sofa. He picked at the crease on his pants leg. "I don't think I'll ever be able to look at the deceased the same way again."

"I don't blame you," Danny said, only half-intending the words to be spoken aloud.

"Who would know that these men weren't to be embalmed?" Audrey asked.

Greenspan frowned and gave them both a slightly condescending look. "Well, anyone with any familiarity with our burial customs who read the obituaries, I suppose."

Suddenly, Danny didn't feel quite so kindly disposed toward Mr. Greenspan. He was just like the funeral home, as it turned out. Meticulous in presentation, but fundamentally grim and pragmatic. Once the veneer of pleasantry had been rubbed off, he was far less genteel. Which made Danny wonder what else might be hiding beneath that veneer.

Audrey began to ask another question, but Danny interrupted.

"Had you ever met Detective Castillo before he came to question you in this matter?"

"Of course not," Greenspan scoffed. "He was a detective in Boston, yes? This is Watertown. I certainly haven't had occasion to be involved in any *other* murder investigations."

There was a moment's pause as they all digested both question and answer. Then Audrey went on, inquiring about Greenspan's knowledge of both the Cohen and Shefts families. Danny knew she would pay particular attention to the Shefts family, since they hadn't allowed the exhumation to go through. But he didn't think it would come to anything.

As far as he was concerned, the entire visit was a waste of time. But they wouldn't have known that if they hadn't come.

Greenspan was putting on airs about it being unprofessional of him to gossip about his clients—though Danny figured he'd do just that if pressed—when Audrey's beeper went off. The two detectives glanced at one another, then Audrey snapped the beeper off her belt and handed it to him. Danny checked the number, and then shot Greenspan a questioning look.

"Back through the viewing area," the man said, obviously dismayed that they should have to use his phone.

"There's a door by the rear exit, next to the rest room. It's a small study, there for the convenience of our clients. There's a phone."

Danny didn't thank him. "Be right back," he said, and went off in search of the hidden phone.

It took him nearly a minute to get Lieutenant Gonci on the line.

"What is it, Loo?"

"You done there?"

"Just about. I don't think we've got anything here. Not unless there's some history between Castillo and this Greenspan, the director here, that we don't know about. I still don't think Castillo's connected at all, actually. I mean, he is now. But I'm wondering if it isn't something done *to* him, instead of *by* him, y'know?"

"It's all theories at this point, Danny," Gonci said. "Hang it up there now."

The tone did it. Danny knew the lieutenant wouldn't have called if there wasn't something major going on, but he wasn't sure how bad it was, exactly, until he heard it in the man's voice.

"We've got somewhere else to be, I take it?"

"Shefts is dead. Tried robbing Somerset Savings and went down hard. But he took some civilians with him."

"Damn!" Danny swore. "There goes one of the only two guys who might have answers on this. I don't suppose Castillo was with him?"

"No sign of Castillo. But actually, there's someone else you might want to question. That's why you're not going to the bank. Head over to SMC; interview a patient there, Timothy Parish."

"What's he got to do with it?" Danny asked, frowning. "One of the victims from the bank?"

Gonci paused. When he spoke again, he sounded almost amused. "Actually, he died on Saturday night. That fraternity party. You remember the case?"

Danny did remember. Jenna had tried to resuscitate the guy. But she'd been unable to do so. He was DOA.

"*Another* one?" Danny asked, bewildered.

"Oh, yes. And I haven't told you the most interesting part. This dead kid came back to life during his autopsy."

When Danny walked back into the sitting room where Audrey was speaking with Greenspan, he looked pale and confused. His partner glanced up at him, and immediately stood up. Audrey cut Greenspan off in mid-sentence, handed him a card with a number where they could be reached, and they were out the door and in the car, on the road back to Somerset before she even asked him what was going on.

After he told her, Audrey could only swear in a voice just a little above a whisper, and stare out at the road in front of her.

In the administrative wing on the second floor of Somerset Medical Center, Jenna sat at her desk in the M.E.'s office and sipped idly at an iced cappuccino she hadn't really wanted. Across from her, Dyson sat at his own desk, trying to do paperwork but quite obviously getting nowhere with it. In the interior office, Slick sat quietly listening to Charlie Parker's wild horn improv and skimming through medical textbooks with about the same chaotic rhythm.

When Dyson cleared his throat, Jenna jumped, startled.

"You don't have to stay, if you don't want to," he offered. "I'm sure Dr. Slikowski would understand. It's getting late."

Jenna stared at him. "You think I'm worried about missing dinner at the dining hall?" she asked with incredulity. "Come on, Al. I just saw a—"

Dyson held up a finger. "We agreed not to talk about it until we had some information from the lab."

"Right." She nodded solemnly. "Anyway, I'm not going anywhere. I'm back and I'm in this. Am I freaked? Duh. Aren't you? But we're going to figure out what this is all about."

"Should I order pizza?" Dyson asked, a wan attempt at a smile on his face.

"How about Tex-Mex?"

The phone rang suddenly, making them both jump this time. Dyson laughed, embarrassed, and glanced at his phone. Jenna looked at her own phone. It was Slick's direct line. Inside the office, the music was turned down and they heard him answer. After a few muted responses, he hung it up again. Together, they watched the door to his office expectantly.

Momentarily, he appeared in the doorway, hands on the wheels of his chair.

"The boy's system was full of a poison called tetrodotoxin, and traces of several others," the medical examiner said. "The path lab is working on trying to trace possible origins, but there seems little doubt he was poisoned."

Before either Jenna or Dyson could reply, there was a knock at the door. Slick glanced at Dyson, who stood and went to open the door. Detectives Gaines and Mariano entered, looking just as grim as Jenna had ever seen them. When Danny saw her, he smiled politely, but the circumstances didn't allow for more than the most perfunctory greeting.

Which is fine. I'm over him. I'm falling in love with Damon.

It was true. She had no doubt of that. Or perhaps only the slightest glimmer of doubt, when she saw the set of Danny's jaw and the grave look in his eyes.

"Thank you for coming by, Detectives," Slick said.

"Actually, thank you all for sticking around," Audrey replied. "We'll need to talk to you all about what happened today." Then she focused. "And, Jenna? We'll want to talk to you about Saturday night."

When I tried to save his life, and couldn't, and he died, she thought. *Only he didn't. Did he?*

For the next twenty minutes, Jenna and Slick and Dyson answered the detectives' questions. It was obvious to Jenna that it wasn't much help to them, but she could have told them that from the outset. What had happened that day was impossible, or should have been. Yet, while the others searched for a logical, scientific explanation, Jenna's mind went back to the morgue the day before, where Jason Castillo had also risen from the dead. She shivered as she recalled the chanting ritual she had heard, and the vacant, sluggish expression on Castillo's face.

"Jenna? Something on your mind?" Audrey asked.

"Huh?"

"You had a look," the detective went on. "I've seen it before. Like you just thought of something."

"I was thinking about yesterday," she explained, glancing from face to face in that room. People she liked. People she trusted. Even Audrey, who had been very curt with her when it seemed as though something might be happening with Danny, but who seemed fine now.

Dyson shifted uncomfortably. "I've been trying *not* to think about yesterday."

Jenna looked at him. "Remember the voice? Chanting, or whatever?" She turned to Danny and Audrey. "We heard it, in the morgue. Like some kind of spell. And then . . . the way Detective Castillo looked, almost like he'd had a lobotomy or something."

Dyson sat up a bit straighter. "But Parish wasn't that way at all," he said, realizing what she was getting at. "He was in pain, and bewildered, but . . . aware."

Jenna nodded. "He was Tim Parish still. I never met Detective Castillo before, but there was definitely something wrong with him. That wasn't the case with Tim."

"So whatever was done to the detective to bring him out of that deathlike state was not done to the Parish boy," Dr. Slikowski said thoughtfully. "With that much toxicity in his system, he ought to have died. The doctors treating him believe that the shock of pain from my incision may actually have saved his life by, in a sense, jump-starting brain activity."

Jenna frowned. She stared at Slick. "That all sounds

great. I'd like to think that's all true, and it does kind of fit with what we've got. But I'm not sure I buy it."

"You'd rather believe in zombies?" Danny asked, a half smile on his face.

"No," she said defensively. "But I'd like to know how a hospital full of doctors sends a body down to the morgue when the patient isn't really dead." Jenna turned to Slick. "*You* didn't even notice."

"Even Einstein made mistakes," Dyson said.

"Great. Good. Can we just hurry up and figure out how all this is being done, then? I know I'd sleep better."

Slick wheeled his chair closer to her. "That's what we're all doing, isn't it? Believe me, I want to get to the bottom of this as much as anyone." He glanced at the detectives. "The poison is a good place to start. Tetrodotoxin isn't something you come across on the average college campus."

Jenna chuckled dryly at that, and the others looked at her.

She shrugged. "The way things have been going around here, I hope to hell Somerset isn't the average college campus."

chapter 10

"Since nobody else is going to say this, I guess it's up to me." Yoshiko looked sheepishly around the room. Then she stared at Jenna. "Maybe going back to that job was a bad idea?"

Damon and Hunter both grinned, even chuckled, and then tried to hide the fact that they'd done so. Jenna shot them both a withering glance and then turned to Yoshiko, a bit taken aback.

"That isn't fair," she said. "You know how hard this was for me. Okay, it's weird and it's crazy, but it isn't just about that. It means something to me."

"You left out dangerous," Damon said, all trace of humor gone from his face. He looked at her gravely and slipped his arm around her, where they sat together on the floor of Sparrow 311, leaning against Jenna's bunk. "You just started back, Jenna, and now . . . two days in a row, you have this insanity."

Jenna sighed. "And you're worried about me. I know.

So are my parents. So am I. But it's what I want to do. It feels right and important. It feels like it matters. So maybe I could get a little support here instead of a hard time?"

Damon said nothing more. Instead, he leaned in and kissed her softly. After the kiss, Jenna looked at Hunter and Yoshiko, who were sitting together on the wide wooden shelf beneath the windows. Hunter pressed his lips together to indicate that he hadn't said and wouldn't say anything to argue the point.

Yoshiko didn't seem quite as cooperative.

"It's important to you, absolutely," she said, leaning forward to emphasize her words. "But you're important to us. And your life should be important to *you*."

Yoshiko fairly floated in the Irish wool sweater she wore, and it made her seem almost like a little girl. But Jenna knew if she mentioned it, Yoshiko would only get angry. She was being serious. Almost too serious, particularly tonight, when they'd vowed not to study or do anything at all responsible.

After the day that Jenna had had, and the pressure they all felt as finals approached, they wanted a little time to themselves—which had required pizza, an enormous bag of Smartfood popcorn, and much caffeine. And a movie, of course. Hunter had rented one of his favorites, *The Outlaw Josey Wales*. Despite Jenna's complaint of possible testosterone overload, she had loved it. They all had.

But once it was over, the conversation went right back to the bizarre developments in the case Jenna had been working on. After all, they'd all been there when Tim

Parish had apparently died, and it was difficult for them to imagine that his death was exactly that—apparent.

"If you really intend to keep at your job—and I guess, knowing how you feel about it, I can't really blame you—couldn't you at least try to keep the job at the hospital, just stick with the clinical stuff?"

"I could," Jenna said, nodding. "But I don't want to."

They all stared at her.

"I guess I'm not following that," Damon said, his fingers rubbing the nape of her neck.

It was a distraction, but a pleasant one. She looked at him a moment before replying, and rested her right hand on his leg. It felt nice to be close to him, even if she didn't like the confused look on his face.

"I'm on the team," she said, realizing how weak it sounded. "Dr. Slikowski is a brilliant man, but he's also just as obsessive, in his own way, as I am. Something like this comes up, he doesn't like to just sit and wait for the cops to solve it. When they ask him to consult on something, he loves it, the challenge. If he asks me to go with him to a crime scene, or wants to talk about a case, I can't say no to that. Even if he doesn't ask, if something gets my attention like that, I can't just shut off my interest in it, my fascination, y'know? My head doesn't work that way."

They all stared at her.

Yoshiko smiled. "Well, I guess we all knew that."

Jenna nodded, relieved.

"So what are you going to do?" Hunter asked. "I mean, if Dr. Slikowski and the cops and everybody are working it, what's your angle gonna be?"

"Tim Parish, I guess," Jenna said. "If I can figure out how whatever happened to him happened to him, or where or why or whatever . . . though I'd guess the police will be looking pretty heavily into that anyway."

"Zombies," Hunter suggested.

"Hunter, come on," Damon chided him.

Yoshiko gave him a little smack. "You know there's no such thing. Really. I mean, I know what you said about voodoo and everything, but this is something else. If these people were really zombies, Tim Parish wouldn't be alive right now."

"Whatever," Hunter said, and shrugged with a bit of embarrassment. "I just think that every legend had to start somewhere. Maybe there's no such thing as a real zombie, like the walking dead and such. But all this stuff sounds an awful lot like the stories I heard when I was a kid. If I was gonna look into this, I reckon I know where I'd start."

"Did you just say 'I reckon'?" Damon asked, incredulously. "I am never letting you watch a western again."

Hunter grinned and gave Damon the finger. They all laughed. Except for Jenna. She was looking at Hunter, brow furrowed in contemplation. When Hunter noticed her scrutiny, he stopped laughing, and looked around guiltily.

"Did I say something you're going to hurt me for?" he asked fearfully.

"Nope," Jenna replied, broken from her concentration. She stood up and went over to give Hunter a hug and a kiss on the forehead. "Just the opposite. Maybe my problem all along has been that I've been dismissing the idea of zombies, instead of trying to see past all the legends and stories."

Jenna went to her computer and logged on to the Internet. Yoshiko, Hunter, and Damon gathered around her chair and watched with great interest as she began her research.

"Zombies," Damon muttered under his breath. "Gotta say, J. Half the thrill going out with you is never knowing exactly what's going to happen next."

Jenna grinned, even as she stared at her computer screen. "What's the other half?"

Yoshiko and Hunter glanced at Damon, who leaned forward to kiss the top of Jenna's head.

"Tell you later," he promised.

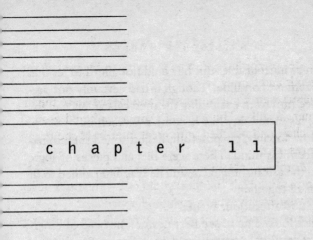

It snowed on Wednesday morning. A dusting, really, but enough to nearly cover the brittle, frozen grass on the quad and frost the skeletal trees all over campus. Enough to serve as a reminder that December had just now arrived, and a long winter lay ahead.

Dr. Slikowski propelled his wheelchair along the paved path between the medical school and Somerset Medical Center, the narrow wheels leaving a double stripe on the tar. He had given a lecture at the med school, but had found that his mind was elsewhere. The bizarre circumstances of the previous week had begun to wear on him. Impossibility piled upon impossibility, and a great many people were looking to him to bring reason and science to it all.

He had no doubt he would do just that. But for the moment he still allowed himself the luxury of bafflement. It was the simplest response, to be so amazed by a set of circumstances as to allow one's mind to see them as inexplicable. But he could not afford to let that amazement continue. Though it had certainly not prevented him from examining the medical evidence in the case, his incredulity had become a distraction.

Now, forcibly, purposefully, he jettisoned such thinking from his mind. There were bits and pieces of logic amid the astonishing facts, and he was determined to fit them all together.

"Good afternoon, Walter."

Slick looked up to see Bert Levine, the head of emergency services, sipping a cup of coffee and looking at him expectantly.

"Oh, hello, Bert," he said, brushing melting snowflakes from his hair. "Sorry. Head in the clouds. How are you?"

"I'll be better once I know this resurrection business is over," Levine said, obviously exasperated. "If one more person asks me about it, I swear I'm taking a month off."

"Is it really that bad?" Slick asked, surprised. "I thought the administration was working with the police to keep the details quiet."

"They're failing," Levine said bluntly. "If they want to avoid a media circus on this thing, they'd better hurry and get to the bottom of it."

Slick smiled politely, or tried to, hoping the expression didn't appear as false as it felt. *They*, Levine had said. But Slick heard *you*, instead. Still attempting to be sociable, he excused himself as courteously as possible and headed for the elevator, even more intent on his purpose now. As he rode up to the second floor, he removed his wire-rimmed glasses and wiped them on his jacket.

The door to his second-floor office was locked. He'd known Dyson would be otherwise engaged that afternoon, but Slick was surprised that Jenna had not arrived yet, as it was half past two. He unlocked the door and turned on the light, then propelled his chair across the room to his interior office. There would be no need to dig out the case files; he had never put them away. His other duties were not neglected—he attended to his lectures and the necessary autopsies with the utmost professionalism—but already he had been asked to consult on two other cases that week and had politely declined.

Before moving behind his desk, Slick put on a Charlie Parker CD. He'd been listening to Bird an awful lot lately, and he thought this case had something to do with that. There was something frenetic about Parker's music that kept him on edge, gave him a kind of momentum.

With Charlie Parker's wild horn resounding through the office, Slick wheeled himself back behind his desk and began to examine the files on Cohen, Shefts, Castillo, and particularly the Parish boy, yet again. The lab results had come in that morning, but he had a hard time making any sense of them. There was poison involved, he knew that. But according to the toxicologist, it wasn't any conventional poison.

Slick was deep in thought when something moved just beyond his peripheral vision. Before he could even look up, a thin, musty, leather-bound book landed on his desk with a slap.

"Sorry I'm late," Jenna said.

"God, Jenna, you gave me a start."

She smiled and shrugged slightly. "Sorry. Never thought of you as a jumpy kind of guy."

"I'm not jumpy."

"Uh-huh," Jenna said, moving on. She pointed at the slim volume she'd just dropped onto his desk. "I wanted to show you that. I found it in the library at the med school."

Slick frowned, but was unable to hide his amusement. He had grown quite fond of Jenna, and he admired her as well. But at times like this, he was reminded even more strongly than usual how young she was. He thought it likely that she'd startled him on purpose, and yet couldn't find any fault in her for it. Dr. Slikowski had no children of his own, and he had wondered, once or twice, if they might have turned out a bit like Jenna: bright and impetuous. He liked to think so.

Rolling his eyes toward heaven, he uttered a small sigh at the smirk on her face, and picked up the book. Its title alone was more reading than some people did in a day: *Our Home Doctor: Domestic and Botanical Remedies, Simplified and Explained, For Family Treatment, With a Treatise on Suspended Animation, the Danger of Burying Alive, and Directions for Restoration.*

All trace of amusement left him. Slick looked up at Jenna doubtfully. "You're joking, aren't you?" When she did not respond immediately, he glanced at the title page. The book had been written by a local doctor and published by a small Boston firm in 1886. He fanned a few of the early pages and found it to be precisely what he expected: the best explanation the times could offer for premature burial.

"This sort of thing was common in the nineteenth century," he told her. "Feeding the populace's fear of premature burial developed into an industry unto itself."

Jenna only nodded and slid into the chair opposite Slick's desk. She leaned over and picked the book up, then held it up so that he could see the cover clearly again.

"Of course, science, since then, has rationally explained all of the crazy things we'd find in here, right?" she asked.

Her eyes seemed to search his face for some sign, some answer she needed quite desperately.

"Of course," Slick agreed.

"But the doctor who wrote that sounds pretty convincing. What little of it I've read. He thought he knew all there was to know about medicine and modern science."

Slick raised his eyebrows, and stared at her. After a moment, he began to smile. At length, he leaned back in his wheelchair and shook his head.

"Once again, our minds work along the same lines," he said. "I've just been thinking about exactly that, banishing preconceptions to make way for the rational scientific explanation of what's been going on here."

It was Jenna's turn to look pleasantly surprised. "Which is?"

Slick's expression became troubled. "I don't know yet." He glanced at her sharply. "Do you?"

"Nope," she said freely. "But I'm willing to bet there's a preconception you're still working under that's preventing you from looking at this thing clearly."

"Please do go on," the M.E. replied amiably.

"Zombies."

Exasperated, Slick sighed. "Come on, Jenna. Please don't start that again. There are no such things as zombies."

Jenna nodded, her expression grave now. "I never said there were." Then she tossed the book back onto Slick's desk. "But there's a reason this book was written. And there's got to be a reason people believe in zombies, right?"

For a seemingly interminable moment, he only looked at her. Then he hung his head a moment, a self-deprecating smile on his face.

"You're right. I haven't been looking at this clearly," he admitted. Then he wheeled himself out from behind the desk and into the outer office, not waiting for Jenna to follow. "Log on to the Internet, please, Jenna."

"This is incredible," Jenna said, staring at the computer screen.

Behind her, Dr. Slikowski sat in his wheelchair, nodding slowly. "Indeed. But it all begins to make sense now, doesn't it? Thanks to your little excursion over to the med school to pick up that antique."

Jenna smiled, though she knew Slick was overstating facts quite a bit. She had made him realize that he was not looking at the entire picture, given him the piece of the puzzle that he was missing. But this was one puzzle she never could have solved on her own. In addition to the medical reports, themselves rife with terms and shorthand unfamiliar to her, there was too much talk of plants and fish and toxins and—amazing to even consider—voodoo traditions. But the research, once begun, had quickly progressed.

In truth, it had sped along to one, inescapable conclusion.

"Zombies," Dr. Slikowski grumbled. "Extraordinary."

An hour later, Danny Mariano and Audrey Gaines were there, watching the M.E. expectantly as he spoke quietly on the phone in his office. As he talked, he sifted through some papers on his desk. Jenna was at her cubicle, and only smiled nervously when either of the detectives looked at her.

"Jenna, come on," Danny said after they had waited several minutes. "What's going on? We're under a lot of pressure, here. If you guys have a lead, let's have it. Otherwise, we really should—"

"Danny, just . . . just wait, okay?" she asked. "Really, I'd tell you myself, but I think you need to hear it from him. I tried to explain it to Al Dyson on the phone, and he thought I was making it up, so just give him a minute, okay?"

"Well, I'm intrigued," Audrey said lightly.

Her partner crossed his arms and settled back against Dyson's desk, looking curiously at Jenna, who only shrugged again helplessly.

So impatient, Jenna thought. *Maybe it's a good thing we never got together; we're too much alike.*

As they waited, she thought about Dyson's reaction. He had phoned to say he was running late and would see Slick in the morning. They had an autopsy scheduled. But when Jenna had tried to explain what was going on, he'd actually laughed at her, until Slick got on the phone to back her up. She planned to punish Dyson for his lack of faith with relentless teasing, but that would have to wait for a quieter time.

Things were just getting really interesting.

Slick hung up the phone. Quickly, he came around his desk and propelled himself out into the outer office.

"I'm sorry to keep you waiting, Audrey. Danny. But that call was necessary to help me get a little perspective on what I've been able to establish thus far," he said. Then he glanced apologetically at Jenna. "Or, I should say, what *we've* been able to establish."

Audrey smiled fondly. "I'm happy for you, Walter. Maybe you could share it with us?"

Slick nodded. "Yes, of course. Then I'll let you try to convince your lieutenant and your counterparts in our neighboring cities that I haven't completely lost my mind."

"This is getting better every second," Danny said. "Why do I know I'm going to have a headache shortly?"

Jenna chuckled and looked over at Dr. Slikowski. She thought she saw a bit of mischief in his eyes, even a bit of a grin playing at the edges of his mouth.

"We have reason to believe that Jason Castillo is a zombie." Slick paused only a moment, his expression grim now, informing them all exactly how serious he was. "As was Marc Cohen. As was Adam Shefts. As Tim

Parish would have been, if the process by which one apparently can create a zombie had been completed."

Silence. Danny's gaze flicked over to Jenna. This time, she didn't smile either. It was Audrey who spoke first.

"I guess I don't have to ask if this is a practical joke," the detective said. "But maybe you should explain."

Slick nodded, as both detectives pulled chairs over so the four of them sat in a circle, facing one another.

"The woman I just spoke to on the phone, Professor DeLissio, is a tropical ecologist here at Somerset," he began. "She has worked, in her time, with some of the most prominent scientists in her own and other related fields of study, many of them here in Boston. I won't bore you with names or details, but suffice to say, she was able to confirm some things I needed to know for certain.

"Since we have the most complete information on Timothy Parish, let's begin with him. His system was loaded with tetrodotoxin. It seems that goes a long way toward explaining a number of the symptoms he showed when he was pronounced legally dead. There are other things that were found in his system—all of which will be found in my report on this matter—that explain the others."

With a frown, Danny leaned forward. "Dr. Slikowski, come on. The kid was cold to the touch, he had no vitals whatsoever, rigor even set in. You're saying there's a poison that can do that?"

"Not *one* poison," Jenna put in.

Slick smiled at her. "Exactly." He turned to the detectives again. "Researchers in Haiti delved into the secret societies of the voodoo culture there and found that the zombie legends are based on truth. Not that people rise from the dead, of course, although local custom presents it as such. The houngan, or shaman of the voodoo culture, gathers together ingredients from a wide variety of sources—certain plants, puffer fish, a thing called a bouga toad, and human remains—to create a powder which, when introduced into the human body, creates the *illusion* of death."

Jenna's face contorted with disgust. "Can I just say 'gross'? You didn't tell me about the human remains part."

Dr. Slikowski looked at her oddly. "Well, they're an inert element of the powder. It seemed pointless. The other ingredients, however, are all highly toxic."

"I'm missing something," Audrey interjected. "If all of this stuff is so toxic, why don't they die?"

Slick seemed almost pleased with the question. "It's fascinating, actually. By all rights they ought to. Certainly the Parish boy should be dead. Would have been, if the shock of the scalpel hadn't caused a surge of adrenaline to run through his system.

"Autopsies on Cohen and Shefts revealed large amounts of another toxin, called datura, in their bodies. Bizarre as it may seem, I hypothesized—and have since had those hypotheses confirmed by outside sources—that the initial poisoning puts the victim in a deathlike state, and later, the datura is used both to shock the victims into consciousness, and to keep them in a docile, almost trancelike state, during which they are highly suggestible. I believed this is what Adam Shefts was doing to Jason Castillo in the morgue when Jenna and Dr. Dyson came upon them."

"So it's this datura stuff that makes them zombies?" Danny asked doubtfully.

"Or the combination of toxins," Slick confirmed. "In fact, after the ordeal, and suffering the effects of the various toxic substances, they would be likely to know and act upon only the things that were told to them. They would have hardly any grasp of self whatsoever."

Danny nodded slowly. "But the Parish kid never had the datura. So he would've died if you hadn't cut into him."

"I think so, yes," Slick said. "The adrenaline flushed into his system was enough to begin to counteract the first round of toxins. The SMC staff did the rest."

Jenna saw understanding dawn on Audrey's face, and she glanced away in dismay.

"It's like brainwashing," Audrey said, her tone reflecting her own horror. "Or worse. Meaning someone was using Cohen and Shefts to do their dirty work. They had no idea what they were really doing, but they died for it."

Danny leaned back in his chair and grunted unhappily. "So if we run up against Castillo—"

"You'd be up against the victim, not the real criminal," Jenna interrupted, putting voice to what they were all thinking.

"Which means we have to find him before whoever's behind all this can get him into any more trouble," Audrey said. "Poor bastard."

Danny stood up and started to put on his coat. He turned to Slick with a very troubled expression on his face.

"So, are we looking for someone who practices voodoo?" he asked. Then he shook his head before anyone could respond. "No, that'd be too easy, right? We're trying to find someone with access to the information you just gave us, and the ability to put it to use."

The expression on Danny's face, and the look on Audrey's, said it all. But Jenna couldn't help putting it into words anway.

"We know how it's being done," she said. "But we're no closer to figuring out who's actually doing it."

Audrey sighed as she rose to move toward the door with Danny. She paused there and glanced back at Dr. Slikowski. "Walter, would you mind calling Lieutenant Gonci while we're on our way back there? It would probably make our lives easier when we go to try to explain this to him if you took a shot at it first."

"Of course," Slick agreed.

Before closing the door, Danny looked back into the office. He nodded at both of them. "Thank you. At least now we know what we're dealing with. Hopefully we can stop this before anyone else dies."

Neither Slick nor Jenna replied.

She wondered if he kept silent for the same reason she did: Jenna didn't believe for a moment that the killing was over.

Thursday afternoon after class let out, Jenna walked downhill to Clayburn Hall in search of Tim Parish's room. He was still in the hospital—where the police had questioned him relentlessly, trying to figure out how he might have come into contact with what she thought of as the "zombie toxin"—but she thought she might talk to his roommate. She'd tried calling, but only got the machine, and didn't want to leave a message. When she got to his dorm room, though, there was no one around. She was about to leave when a tall, sort of fidgety guy came toward her down the corridor.

"Hi," he said nervously. "Can I help you with something?"

Jenna smiled uncertainly, then it clicked. She gestured back at the door. "Your room?"

Mr. Fidgety nodded, trying on a smile as if it wouldn't fit.

"So you're Tim's roommate?"

"Bart," the guy said, nodding.

"I'm Jenna." She held out her hand, and he shook it, looking at her fingers as though she might squeeze too hard.

She wasn't sure exactly how to approach him, so she decided to play it coy. "Is Tim around?" she asked.

"He's still in the hospital," Bart told her.

Jenna learned a lot at that moment. Bart's tone told her that he didn't much want to talk about Tim, that maybe he didn't really like Tim all that much. It only reinforced how lucky she'd always felt to be paired up with Yoshiko. Bart was a mess of nerves, as her mother would have said. Jenna wondered if he was always like that, or just around girls.

Or maybe he's hiding something.

"Oh," Jenna said, nodding sagely. "Yeah, I guess he would be. What a weird thing, huh? I mean, how does that happen? One second you're dead, and then you're not? It's almost like he was a vampire or something. Or a zombie."

As she said this last, Jenna watched Bart carefully. She knew she wasn't much of an actress, and the words had felt forced to her, but he didn't seem to react at all, except to nod in agreement.

"Pretty freaky," Bart conceded. "I guess the cops think someone did it to him on purpose, too."

"No kidding?" she said.

"Yep. Came in with a warrant just this morning and searched the room and everything."

She smiled at him. "Wow. That had to be weird. Listen, I'll just come by again when he's out of the hospital. How long do you think it'll be?"

"Couple more days, I guess," Bart said, but it was clear he didn't really know.

"Thanks, Bart. I appreciate it."

He said nothing as she walked away. Only when she was near the door to the stairs did he manage to respond. "Any time!"

Jenna grinned as she went down the stairs.

She didn't know what the Somerset P.D. had made of Bart, but she scratched him off her mental list of suspects. Sure, he could have cleaned out the room before the cops got there, but it would have been hard for him to do anything truly weird with Tim around, and besides, he seemed like just a sweet, geeky guy.

Definitely didn't have that criminal mastermind vibe.

Still, though, Jenna felt like she needed to do something, so she walked across campus toward Delta Tau Delta. On the way, she turned the situation over and over in her mind. It was easy to understand the logic behind what had happened to Cohen and Shefts. They were Orthodox Jews, and therefore wouldn't be embalmed. They could be—what, enslaved?—pretty easily, and no one would be the wiser. With Castillo, it was a matter of getting him out of the way.

But why Tim?

Logic brought her around to the realization that Tim had to have had contact, no matter how unintentional, with the powder. That meant he had likely had contact with whoever was making the powder and was behind the robberies and murders. The kid had no idea how lucky he was to have survived.

If the cops had searched Tim's room, that probably meant that they had come to the same conclusion. It also meant they'd be questioning Tim, and most of his friends. More than likely, they'd search DTD as well.

It might not be the best time to drop in unannounced.

After all, she had been warned by everyone, from her parents to Slick to Hunter and Yoshiko to Damon, not to stick her nose in. If she started asking questions around DTD and the answers were what she suspected they might be, she would just be asking for trouble.

But, soon enough, she found herself on the front steps of the frat house, ringing the bell.

There was shouting inside, a couple of guys yelling at each other to answer the door. *One of you answer,* Jenna thought. *Before I freeze to death.* She shivered a bit as a cold wind blew down Sterling Lane. Finally the door was yanked open by a guy Jenna didn't recognize.

"Hey," he said, giving her the once-over. "Help you with something?"

He had a rugged thing going on that Jenna found pretty appealing—the whole grrrr factor—but also a swagger she didn't like. Unfortunately, she'd found that swagger pretty common among both fraternity guys and jocks. Not universal, by any means, but common neverthless.

"Yeah, hi, I was looking for Tim Parish," Jenna lied, smiling. "Is he here?"

The guy seemed unsure for a second, and then he nodded. "Right. Tim. Pledge. Resurrection man. I think he's still in the hospital, but you're welcome to look. Come on in."

He stood aside and Jenna entered. The second she was inside, the guy left her to her own devices. She felt very awkward, cast adrift in the midst of a fraternity house, but she walked toward the back of the house, where she thought she remembered seeing the kitchen the last time she'd been there. She found the kitchen all right, but it was empty.

"Can I help you?"

Jenna spun around, a bit startled, but was happy when she saw Ed Switzer. "Ed, hey."

"Sorry," he said, friendly enough. "Have we . . . ?"

"Oh, no, not really. I'm a . . . I mean, I was a friend of

Melody LaChance. I think we met once, briefly. My name's Jenna Blake."

Ed narrowed his eyes, just for a second. Then he nodded. "Wait, Jenna? The girl who works for the coroner."

"Medical examiner," she corrected, rolling her eyes and smiling in self-deprecation. "But yeah, that's me. I hate to think that's how people know me, though."

"Nah, pretty cool," Ed reassured her. "Hey, that really sucked with Melody. She was a sweetheart."

"Yeah," Jenna agreed, and then fell silent a moment, remembering.

"Hey, anyway, what brings you to our humble asylum?"

"I was looking for Tim Parish," she said. "He's a pledge, I guess."

Ed frowned. "Tim's still in the hospital."

"Oh," Jenna replied, not quite certain what to say next. "I figured he'd be out by now. So weird what happened with him, wasn't it?"

"More than weird," Ed said. "Like a miracle or something."

Jenna swallowed nervously. "Would you mind if I asked you some questions about that?"

"What for?" he asked suspiciously.

"For the M.E., actually. We're wondering if anyone else has shown any kind of odd symptoms, if there's a specific kind of food or something that might be to blame. Just exploring every angle."

He studied her a moment, then shrugged. "Yeah, I guess. Look, though, Vic's upstairs. You should talk to him. He's the prez, so he knows much more about what goes on around here."

"That'd be great," Jenna told him, relieved.

Ed went to lead the way, but she hesitated. Ed seemed like a good guy, but she'd seen enough newscasts and read enough papers to know a girl going upstairs in a frat house was a bad idea. Again, the thought that she was unfairly generalizing occurred to her, but then she wondered if it had occurred to girls who had been raped as well.

Ed seemed almost to have read her mind.

"Or, you know what? If you want, why don't you grab a beer or a Coke or something, and I'll see if I can get Vic to come down," he said kindly. "Like he'll argue when I tell him there's a pretty girl looking for him."

Jenna laughed politely, flattered in spite of herself. "That'd be great, thanks."

Then, though she was uncomfortable doing it, she did open the fridge and root around for a soda, ending up with a can of Sprite. As she opened it and sat down at the table—surprised by how clean the kitchen actually was, all things considered—a guy in cutoff shorts and a T-shirt trudged in, a copy of *The Sea Wolf* in his hand. It took Jenna a second to realize it was Brian Duffy, the guy who had tried to start a fight with Hunter and Damon the previous Saturday night, and had yanked her by the hair.

"Oh, hey," Duffy grunted. "Didn't know anyone was in here."

For a moment, she said nothing, just hating him. But then she thought about how drunk he'd been. It didn't give him an excuse, and it didn't mean he wasn't a jerk, but for the moment, he wasn't a drunken jerk.

"Getting ready for the American Lit final?" Jenna asked.

"Huh?" Duffy studied her a little more, then seemed to recognize her. Though it quickly became obvious that he recognized her from class, and not from the party. "Oh, hey," he said. "Yeah. Trying to make some sense of it. So far, Jack London seems like the only one of the writers we're studying who wasn't full of shit."

"That's one way of looking at it," Jenna said, laughing in spite of her distaste for Duffy after his behavior the previous weekend.

Suddenly, he focused on her again. "Hey, wait a second. You were the chick who tried saving Parish's life the other night."

"Do people still say 'chick'?" she asked. When Duffy only looked confused, she nodded. "Yeah, that was me. Lot of good it did him."

"Can't have hurt much," Duffy said with a shrug. "He wasn't really dead after all, right? Could be you saved him and didn't even know it."

Jenna looked at Duffy, surprised to find that when he was sober, he wasn't anywhere near as much of a moron as he'd been at the party. He must have seen some of that in her face, because he smirked.

"Listen, sorry about getting all up in your friend's face at the party. I'm not a good drunk. Never have been."

Before he could continue, Ed appeared once again, with Vic in tow.

"Success!" Ed reported, and went to a cupboard to pull down a bag of pretzels.

"Hi, Vic," Jenna said. "We didn't really meet the other night, but I'm . . ."

"Jenna. I figured," Vic replied. "Damon doesn't talk about much else."

"He better not," Jenna said.

They all chuckled conspiratorially at that.

"Listen, I don't want to disrupt your day at all, guys," she said. "But as I guess most of you know, I work with the medical examiner's office. We're consulting with the police on Tim's case, and I just wanted to talk to you about it a little."

Vic smiled. "Not exactly a slacker, are you? How'd you end up in that job? I'm amazed they'd let a college freshman do something like that."

"Lucky, I guess," Jenna replied.

"Yeah, playing with dead guys," Duffy cracked. "I guess it depends how you define luck."

It was a cut, but not really a harsh one. When the guys laughed, Jenna laughed along with them.

"So what can I do for you?" Vic asked.

"Well, as I told Ed, we're looking into whether anyone else has had any strange illnesses, and trying to figure out if there might be an environmental cause to what happened with Tim. Food, water, airborne toxins, anything. Y'know, covering all the bases."

Vic narrowed his gaze as he studied her. "Nah. None of that. Nobody else has been sick that I know of. I mean, except for the flu. I think if anybody else died and came back to life, I'd have noticed."

Jenna flushed, feeling silly. "Of course," she said. "It's just that, well, if Tim ate or drank anything, or came into contact with anything that might have—"

"Know what, Jenna?" Vic interrupted. "We spent all morning dealing with the cops on this stuff. I missed classes. They searched the whole damn house, and asked me some really freaky questions. Asked everyone, in fact. No offense, you seem very sweet, but I'm kinda done with that."

Duffy and Ed had fallen silent. Jenna glanced at them, shifting uncomfortably.

"What kind of freaky questions?" she asked.

"One of 'em asked me if I knew anything about voodoo," Duffy volunteered. "You believe that?" He looked at Vic. "They ask you that one, too?"

"Yeah," Vic said sternly. "They did."

Don't say it, Jenna thought. *Just . . . don't . . .*

"What was your answer?" she asked.

Instantly, Jenna regretted it. It was only that they had been so friendly at first, and made her feel comfortable. Now, though, the temperature in the room seemed to drop. Vic frowned, then gave a small laugh that was painfully false. Beyond him, Ed and Duffy were looking at her oddly as well; both of their smiles had disappeared.

Of course they're looking at you like that. They think you're completely wacked now.

"Anyway," she said, "that's really it. If nobody else was affected, there probably wasn't an environmental cause. Thanks, though."

Smiling weakly, she said her good-byes and got out of

the house as quickly as possible. It would have been easy for her to write off their reaction. It *was* a weird question, and they'd been dealing with the cops all morning.

But in her heart, she wondered if there was more to it. The change in the room's atmosphere had been significant. By the time she was walking back up the hill, she had come to believe that the expressions on their faces hadn't merely been caused by surprise or doubt, but by hostility.

It might just be paranoia on her part, she knew.

But past experience had taught her one lesson above all others.

Just because you're paranoid, doesn't mean they *aren't* out to get you.

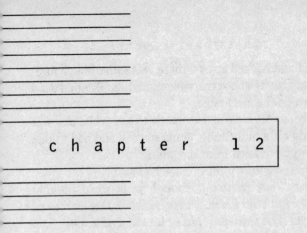

chapter 12

A scalpel glides through most human organs clean as a laser, though the heart is often an exception. Jenna had seen Dyson cut tissue samples from organs during dozens of autopsies, but only once or twice had she done any of the cutting herself. On Friday afternoon, however, she arrived at work to discover that Dyson hadn't shown up at the office that morning. Nor had he called. Her concern was interrupted all too quickly by the news that she would be assisting—truly assisting— Dr. Slikowski during the scheduled autopsy.

The subject of the autopsy was a woman named Kara Spindler, who had apparently driven her car into a pond in Medford. Of course, *apparently* was the operative word. The medical examiner had to autopsy anyone who died suspiciously or violently, and Kara Spindler fit both categories.

Though Jenna had seen things while working for Slick that were stomach-churning—people beaten and burned and hacked apart—there was something haunting and ghastly about the wide-eyed, blue-skinned dead woman on the steel table.

Once, as Slick turned to speak to her while she was slivering off a bit of lung, Jenna started, and had to bite her tongue to keep from screaming.

"You're awfully jumpy," Slick had said.

"Sorry," she muttered, though what she'd thought was, *She just looks frozen. Frozen, but alive. Like any second she might start screaming, just sit up and scream, like . . .*

Jenna couldn't even finish the thought for herself, but she didn't have to. *Like Tim Parish,* that was where her mind was going. The memory of Tim snapping awake, coming to life like that, would not leave her. The dead woman had her abdomen sliced open and pinned back, half her skull off, her organs arrayed about the room. But in the back of Jenna's mind, there was a quaver of fear that Kara Spindler wasn't dead after all.

Crazy. She knew that but it didn't help, not with the cold, dead eyes in the blue, frosted skin.

Now the scalpel in her hand neatly sectioned a sample of liver tissue, and she tried not to look at the dead woman's face. When Slick spoke to her again, it took her a moment to register his words.

"It's certainly an avenue worth pursuing, Jenna," he said. "But I think this time around we'd best confine our theories and investigations to paper and computers."

Jenna frowned, a bit surprised. She had told Dr. Slikowski about her excursion to Delta Tau Delta, and had expected him to chide her for it. But generally when she did such things, his admonitions contained a kind of tacit approval. He wished he could do the same; at times, he actually *did*.

"I really didn't know what I'd find," she said in her defense. "It was just a hunch."

Slick glanced at her, his expression unreadable behind the white mask he wore. "I'm not saying I don't want to go beyond the call of duty, Jenna. We've talked about it before, how much we both relish the challenge, the puzzle involved in a case like this. But I want to make sure we keep a safe distance this time. You quit on me the last time you got too close to a case."

"That won't happen again," she said, somewhat sullenly.

With one gloved hand, Slick pulled the mask down off his face to reveal the warm smile there. "I hope not. But I don't want you to put yourself at risk. You had a hunch, and you followed it. But as you learned, the police had been there ahead of you. Let Gaines and Mariano do their jobs, and we'll just play Jiminy Cricket for them, all right?"

Jenna nodded. "I kind of like the Danny-as-Pinocchio image."

They went back to work, but the moment Slick had turned his attention back to the dead woman's open skull, he spoke again.

"So, you think one of the fraternity brothers is responsible?"

Jenna took a long breath. "Maybe. Or maybe all of them. I don't know. It's possible I imagined the whole thing. Creepy feelings and bad attitudes are hardly evidence of murder."

"No," Slick agreed.

"But, speaking of creepy feelings . . ." Jenna let the words trail off.

Slick's hands stopped moving. He glanced up at her again and pushed his wheelchair back from the table just a bit. "You're worried about Dr. Dyson," the M.E. said. It wasn't a question.

"So are you," Jenna replied. "You called him?"

"Several times. Feel free to try again."

"Did you call Doug?"

Behind his wire-rimmed glasses, Dr. Slikowski's eyes widened a bit. "I honestly hadn't thought of that. Nor do I have a number. Though I don't think Al Dyson is the type to play hooky."

"Neither do I," Jenna agreed.

That's the problem. If she thought Dyson was lounging around in bed all day with Doug, she'd be happy for him, instead of worried. *But that's not Dyson.*

Jenna stripped off her gloves and tossed them into the hazardous waste bin. Then she went to the phone and dialed information. She didn't remember the number offhand, but she knew Doug lived in Boston. It was a simple matter to get the number from information.

"Hello?"

"Doug, hi. This is Jenna Blake."

"Hi, Jenna. This is a surprise. What's up?"

She took a breath. Dared to hope. "Is Al there?"

There was a pause on the other end of the line. Then Doug cleared his throat. "He's not at work?"

Doug hadn't seen Dyson since the previous morning, nor heard from him since dinner that night.

"I'm sure he's fine," Jenna said, trying to convince herself. "I mean, I guess it's possible he had planned to take today off, and there was just a miscommunication or something."

But Doug didn't seem convinced either. "Please ask him to call me if you hear from him," he asked. "Of course I'll do the same."

"I will," Jenna promised. "Thanks."

When she turned around to face Slick, she could see the concern etched on his face. Under normal circumstances, she knew, neither of them would have been all that concerned. It happened; people made mistakes, or just needed a mental health day. That was what they'd both been telling themselves thus far. But if Doug thought Dyson was at work . . .

"Maybe we should call Danny and Audrey?" she suggested. "I mean, I know he's technically not a missing person yet, and it'll probably sound kind of silly, but . . ." She couldn't put her rationalization into words, so she just shrugged instead.

But Slick understood. "We could at least call them," he said. "Let them know." He pushed his chair up to the autopsy table again. "I'm sure he's fine, Jenna. Really. Let's just finish here, and then I'll phone Audrey."

The rest of the autopsy was completed in relative silence. Slick determined that Kara Spindler had been murdered before someone had put her body in the car and pushed it into the lake.

It was horrible. Her eyes haunting, accusing. But that was the job.

And Dyson was missing.

Jenna called Doug twice on Saturday, and Dr. Slikowski three times. She also spoke to Danny Mariano, who confirmed that they had to wait until Sunday afternoon before they could treat Dyson's disappearance as a missing persons case. She wouldn't have been so concerned if Doug were gone, too. But she had a hard time believing Dyson would just take off without telling anyone. If he wanted a quiet weekend away on Martha's Vineyard or something, he wouldn't have gone without at least telling Doug.

With varying levels of success, she spent most of the day trying not to think about Dyson. Though she never shook her anxiety completely, by six o'clock that night, she had more immediate concerns. Her father and Shayna had asked her to have dinner with them in Boston, and invited Damon along as well. Introducing Dad to the new boyfriend wouldn't have been her first choice of plans for the evening. She was looking forward to it, but she was nervous as well.

A little after six, dressed in black jeans and a pale green cardigan, she walked down the hall to Damon's room, jacket over her arm. The door opened on the first knock, but it wasn't Damon who greeted her.

"Baby J! Smoking, as always." Brick smiled, reached out for her hand, and kissed her knuckles with a flourish worthy of any courtier. Then he turned to look into the room, where Damon and Anthony were flipping through a notebook. "Damon's got too much studying to do, Jenna. I'm afraid I'm gonna have to stand in for him tonight."

Jenna moved into the room and stood next to Brick, their arms comfortably sliding around each other as though they were old friends and co-conspirators.

Damon looked up, his brow furrowed, a dubious smile on his face. "Like hell."

He handed the notebook to Anthony and walked over to Jenna. She thought he looked amazing, more relaxed than most college guys, in wool pants and a collarless shirt. Damon was far better dressed than she was, but that wasn't at all unusual. He gave Brick a playful shove and slipped his arms behind Jenna. Eyes twinkling, he kissed her, and she laughed as he did. It was a perfect moment. For several seconds, it made everything else go away.

After the kiss, their hands stayed loosely entwined.

"You look great," she told him.

Damon grinned. "Time to meet your dad. I want to make a good first impression."

Jenna thought about the first time she'd met him, in the hallway right outside the door. His perfect features and his easy way and his obvious charm had won her over instantly. She suspected that was par for the course for Damon.

"He'll love you."

"Right!" Brick agreed. "What's not to love?" Then he scowled. "Come on, girl, think about it. You're making a big mistake. Sure, he's pretty, but he just doesn't have the mojo, if you know what I mean. You want to impress the old man, I'm telling you, you should bring me along."

Jenna looked doubtfully at Brick, then turned back to Damon. "Did you tell him we were going to the North End?"

Brick looked offended. "All right, I enjoy Italian food. Is that a crime?"

This time, it was Jenna who pushed him. She smiled as she did it, though. Brick loved nothing more than he did the stage, and it showed in his every word. He was a good guy, a good friend, and he had style. Jenna liked him a great deal, and she knew the feeling was mutual. It was easy to like Brick, and she was glad Damon had him for a friend.

Then there was Anthony. The tall, broad-shouldered football player stood across the room, looking at the three of them with an amiable enough smile on his face, but he didn't say a word. Never said much, actually.

"Hey, Ant," Jenna greeted him.

"Jenna," Anthony replied, with the tiniest of nods. That was about it. He went back to reading his notes.

Anthony and Brick were roommates downhill at Bentley Hall, and Jenna couldn't imagine a more mismatched pair.

"You ready to go?" Damon asked.

"Oh yeah."

Downstairs, while they waited for her father and Shayna to pick them up, Jenna updated Damon on the situation with Al Dyson. It wasn't something she wanted to dwell on, but she couldn't help it. Damon's grip on her hand tightened as she spoke.

"He'll be all right," Damon said. "I'm not saying don't be worried. I'm just saying you've gotta have a little faith."

Jenna blinked in surprise and looked at him more closely, wondering if he was talking about God, or just faith in a more general sense. Either way, there was a hope—and yeah, a kind of faith—in his own words that gave her comfort, and made her fondness for him grow even greater.

It was too soon, she thought, for her to be able to say she loved him.

But she thought she might.

Of course, Jenna's father started with the whole "she speaks very highly of you" thing, which seemed so very *Dad* to her, it almost made her forget that he hadn't come by to see her much more often than Santa Claus most of the time she was growing up. It was a nice feeling, and she was surprised to find that it didn't make her bitter at all. Or at least not very.

Shayna smiled and cast an amused glance at Frank when he asked what Damon planned to major in, and if he had any post-college plans as of yet.

"Frank, he's a freshman. Leave him alone," she said.

Jenna tried to thank her telepathically, but didn't think it was working.

For Damon's part, he just looked thoughtful for a moment. He cut a quick glance over at Jenna, and there was a kind of mischief in his eyes that she was becoming very familiar with. But it also worried her. One of her favorite movies was *Say Anything*, with John Cusack, which she'd forced Damon to sit through twice already since they'd met. Under similar circumstances, Cusack's character in the movie, Lloyd, pretty much blows the father/daughter's-new-boyfriend interview. That mischievous twinkle in Damon's eye had her wondering if he would start babbling about kickboxing being the sport of the future, or talking about how he knew he didn't want to buy, sell, or process anything.

Then he stunned her.

"Actually, I think I'd like to teach."

"Really?" Frank replied, smiling. "That's great. There's nothing America needs more than good teachers."

"My father says the same thing," Damon revealed. "He teaches science at my old high school in Jersey."

"So you'd teach science?" Shayna asked with interest.

Damon laughed. "You kidding? I hate science. On the other hand, I love history. Fascinated by it, to tell the truth. Though it's pretty boring to most people, so I don't really talk about it much."

"I guess you don't," Jenna admonished him.

Then she sat and watched in amazement as both her father and Shayna were completely and totally won over by her boyfriend. She had expected them to like him, but this was better than she ever could have hoped. And she'd learned more about him in the bargain. Most freshmen seemed to be just finding their way, to the point where she was almost embarrassed by how directed she herself was.

She hadn't really asked Damon what his plans were because she was so self-conscious about her own. She knew he loved history, but never realized that he meant to pursue a career in academics. They hadn't come far enough along in their relationship that they were comfortable talking about their hopes and dreams with each other just yet, opening up that much.

Suddenly, she found herself wanting more than anything to be alone with him, to ask him more, to find out what else he dreamed of. Under the table, she reached over and grasped his hand, and he gave her fingers a little squeeze.

Later, when they'd finished dinner and were drinking espresso, the talk returned to the subject of Frank and Shayna's upcoming wedding and the sabbatical they would be taking beforehand.

"You two are pretty brave," Damon said with a slight shake of his head.

"What, getting married?" Shayna asked.

"Nah. I mean trying to plan a wedding while you're an ocean away."

Jenna looked at her father, and then at Shayna. Much as she wished they weren't going, she was truly happy for them. With a smile, she leaned toward her father's fiancée.

"You guys *will* have e-mail while you're over there, right? I mean, Dad said you would, but he's a dinosaur, so . . ."

"Of course we will." She laughed.

"Good. That'll make it even easier for me to help. I'm not going to be the wedding planner or anything, but I can do little errands, maybe make some calls, if you need me to."

Jenna glanced at her father. He seemed sad for a moment, and then he grinned. Frank Logan reached for Shayna's hand where it lay on the table, and encircled it with his own.

"That'd be wonderful, Jenna. It means a lot to me that you would offer."

"To both of us," Shayna added.

All in all, it was the nicest time she'd had with her father in a while, maybe even years. After they left the restaurant, Frank and Shayna headed home, but Jenna and Damon stayed in Boston. They walked over to Quincy Market, where Damon bought her a single red hothouse rose on the spur of the moment. It was impractical to walk around with it—the flower would already be suffering from the cold and would die all too quickly. But that sad fact made Jenna appreciate the gesture all the more.

They bought a small bag of still warm chocolate chip cookies at the Boston Chipyard, and ate them right from the bag as they wandered around. They stopped and stole kisses in the least appropriate places, and Jenna didn't care. She smiled a lot, laughed at his charm and his teasing.

No question about it. Much as she wanted to deny it, Jenna knew that she was falling in love with Damon. The romance of that night, just walking around together, only served to make that all the more clear to her. And yet, beneath the surface of what should have been a perfect night, there was an underlying taint to all of it. Dinner with Shayna and her father, and this night with Damon, had made her so happy. But in the back of her mind, almost constantly, were thoughts of the case she'd been working on, of Tim Parish and Jason Castillo.

And of Al Dyson.

When they finally got back to Somerset, Damon walked her to the door of her room, and they shared an intense good night kiss. But she went in alone. She needed sleep, and she needed to think. Yoshiko was fast asleep in the top bunk. Jenna went immediately to the answering machine, and was crestfallen when she saw that there were no messages. Nor had Yoshiko written any down.

Which meant there was still no sign of Dyson.

"You don't think there's any connection to the funeral home, do you?" Danny asked, narrowing his eyes.

Audrey was behind the wheel, but she glanced quickly at him, a troubled expression on her face. "I wouldn't bet the farm, but no, I don't."

"So if we're still going on the assumption that Castillo was taken out because of his investigation, and Shefts and Cohen were used because of their burial customs, that means our only real lead—unless we reinterview every acquaintance of all our 'zombies'—is the Parish kid, right?"

"That's right," Audrey agreed.

"So why are we here instead of hauling every one of those frat boys back to the house for questioning? I mean, a house search and a few Q&A's is not exactly interrogation. Don't you think we should focus a little more?"

"We've been over every guy at DTD. We'll go over them again. For the moment, run with it. Call it a hunch," Audrey told him as she pulled the car up along-side the curb in front of Al Dyson's house.

"What, you think Dyson's in it?" Danny said, incredulously.

They both got out of the car. The previous afternoon, it had become unexpectedly warm for the season, but the rise in temperatures was all too brief. Now it was Sunday morning, and the cold had crept mercilessly back into the air.

Audrey paused on the front walk. "He's a missing person now officially. That means before we do anything else, we need to get into his house to make sure he's not lying dead in there."

All that made perfect sense, but Danny could tell that there was more to it than that. He frowned and stared at Audrey, waiting impatiently.

"Well?" he asked.

"Nothing concrete," she reluctantly admitted. "Just that whoever's behind this probably has some knowledge of medicine. Could even work at a hospital. Is probably around the Somerset area, given that the Parish kid had to come into contact with that powder somehow. You're probably right, Danny. Jenna's probably right. More than likely, it's Parish's freaky roommate, or one of those frat boys. But with Dyson turning up missing, I just thought it was worth a look."

She glared at him. "Now that you've got a thorough explanation of the workings of my brain, can we move on?"

Danny flushed. He hadn't meant to question Audrey's reasoning, just wanted to know what was going on. But he could see how his tone might have insulted her.

"No offense, Aud. You know that. I just hate the weird ones."

"Don't we all."

It was a simple thing to force the door to Dyson's place. They gave it a pretty thorough going over, and came up with nothing. Nearly half an hour after they'd begun, they knew it had been a useless gesture.

"Time to interrogate frat boys?" Danny asked.

Audrey nodded, her expression troubled. "I wish I knew where the hell Dyson got off to. If there were signs of a struggle, it would make more sense."

"One mystery at a time," Danny told her.

Together, they went down the corridor and out into the living room, toward the door. When they were halfway across the room, the front door—which they had closed after forcing their entry—was kicked open with a crash.

On the threshold stood a sickly, dull-eyed Jason Castillo, a gun in his hand.

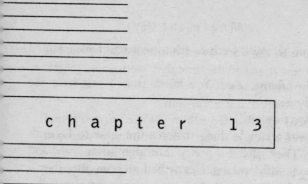

chapter 13

Danny held his breath as he stared at Castillo. There was a vacant, lost look to the other detective's wide-open eyes, and a slackness to his facial muscles that made him look as though he might simply collapse at any moment. But Castillo wasn't going to collapse. The gun was steady in his hand.

It was surreal. On a bright, briskly cold early December morning, they stood in the home of a missing doctor, while one of their own stood before them, a zombie, seemingly back from the dead, ready to shoot them. From behind Castillo, a chill wind rushed through the door, and Danny felt gooseflesh rise on his skin.

One look had told him Castillo wasn't in his right mind. In that same look, Danny knew one other thing for certain: Castillo was there to kill them, and wasn't in any condition to question the instructions he'd been given. It was mere seconds after they'd been confronted at the door by the slack-jawed, entranced detective, but Danny knew it was all the time they were going to get.

He went for his gun.

Audrey stepped in front of him.

"Castillo!" she shouted at him. "Wake up, you stupid son of a bitch! You're a cop! Don't you know who you are? Come on!"

Danny blinked, reared back in astonishment, even as his weapon cleared its holster. If he wanted to shoot Castillo, he couldn't do it with his partner in the way.

"Damn it, Audrey, don't you see his eyes?"

He grabbed her shoulder, attempting to move her back, but she shrugged him off. And Danny had a moment to think that maybe she was right. It was clear to him that she was trying to break through whatever weird brainwashing program Castillo had been put through. She wanted to reach him, try to defuse the situation before someone got killed. It was the right thing to do, the noble thing.

Danny wasn't all that concerned with nobility at the moment. He wanted to stay alive, and he wanted to keep Audrey alive in the bargain. Still, he was slow on the draw as he watched Castillo's reaction. There was no shot, the trigger was not pulled. To his amazement, the entranced cop blinked a couple of times, as if they had flashed bright lights in his face. He took a step back, lowering the gun slightly.

"Jason," Audrey kept on. "That's your name. Jason Castillo. You're a police detective. Someone's done this to you. You've got to wake up."

She didn't want to shoot a fellow cop, especially since

Castillo hadn't actually done anything wrong. Not knowingly.

"Castillo!" Audrey snapped desperately.

Danny couldn't blame her. They wouldn't get a second chance.

But now their first chance was over with. Castillo's eyes lost their momentary alertness; his gaze shifted, slipped out of focus. He raised his weapon.

"Audrey, down!" Danny shouted.

Audrey began to move aside, carefully, so as not to set Castillo off. She didn't seem to realize that it was too late for such precautions. But she had moved just enough.

Even as Castillo brought his weapon to bear, aiming in an almost offhanded way, as if he didn't care whether he hit them at all, Danny brought his own gun up and let off a round. The bullet punched a hole in the door frame just behind Castillo.

It didn't matter.

In that moment the only thing that did matter was getting Audrey out of Castillo's sights. Danny leaped for her, knocked her aside. She stumbled, trying to keep her footing, and then saw the cover that lay ahead of her, and dove behind a high-backed chair in the living room.

In the eyeblink after he shoved Audrey out of the line of fire, Danny was bringing his gun up, ready to get a better shot at the other cop. Even after what had been done to him, even drugged and sluggish and not in his right mind, Castillo was quick.

He pulled the trigger. There was a roar from the barrel of the gun, louder, somehow, than the sound that had come from Danny's own weapon. Louder, perhaps, than any sound he had ever heard before in his life. So loud it seemed to drive him back, seemed to fill him with fire and pain, seemed to leech all the strength from him.

But it wasn't the sound, he realized with sudden, agonized insight.

It was the bullet.

Danny grunted, hissing in pain, clutching at the spot on his lower abdomen where the bullet had passed through. Blood spilled over his fingers, even as he fell. But he did not let go of his gun. Pain forced him to grit his teeth; pain drove him to lift the gun, even as he fell.

His shoulder hit the coffee table on the way down. Another jolt of pain seethed through his body, and now the gun clattered onto the table and then slid off onto the carpet.

Audrey was screaming his name.

Castillo turned his gun on her. Despite the pain of his wound and the fear that he might die, that already his heart might have just stopped, Danny turned his head enough to see the mesmerized detective fire at the chair behind which Audrey ducked. There was a *thunk* as the bullet passed through wood. Castillo fired again, this time shattering the glass covering the fireplace behind Audrey.

Danny saw the blue-gray metal of the barrel of Audrey's gun sliding around the edge of the chair. Then his eyelids fluttered, and he began to lose consciousness.

Jenna had woken up early on Sunday to buckle down in her preparations for exam week. Hunter's roommate wasn't around, so Yoshiko had stayed in *his* room the night before. Jenna didn't know the details, and didn't want to know. The night before, she had told Damon her plans for the day. Though he needed to get some studying done also, he was supposed to hang out with Brick and Ant—some guy thing—and that was all right with her.

Not a whole lot of studying would get done if Damon was around today. The thought made her smile.

Jenna studied for an hour or so, then took a shower. The one thing she wanted to avoid was the typical crunch time slack-off in personal appearance and hygiene that everybody talked about. Granted, it wasn't exam week yet, but upperclassmen she knew had horrified her with stories about not showering for three days, rolling out of bed and going to exams in sweats and in some cases, God forbid, pajamas.

Which was, as Jenna had told them, *wicked gross*.

So after that first round of studying, which had focused on Spanish verb conjugation—a topic certain to make her bleed from her ears and possibly her eye sockets as well—she had wanted to be certain she looked good. Once she had showered, she added a little eyeliner and lip pencil and put on jeans and a deep burgundy sweater. Then she headed over to Keates DH for what they called breakfast. In this case, it was supposed to be scrambled eggs, hash browns, and ham, or something that was dubbed a waffle but—she had learned from brutal experience—actually had the consistency of wet cardboard.

So, scrambled eggs. They had a sort of bland taste to

them, but when slopped on buttered wheat toast and topped with the slice of ham, turned into a passable meal.

After choking that down while her Spanish book was courageously open on the table in front of her, she braced herself for the cold and jogged across the quad toward Sparrow, eagerly anticipating the relative relief of her biology notes. There was no exam in American lit, but a final paper instead. The idea was to discuss the influence of a major American writer, and show how the author's legacy had been furthered by those who came after. Jenna had spent the past month reading and doing research for the topic she'd chosen: "Smarter Than They Look: The Creations and Descendants of Raymond Chandler."

Working on the paper was sheer pleasure. More than that, however, it meant that she only had four classes with finals to study for. She was confident that her European History class wouldn't be a problem, and International Relations was last, so for now, it was Spanish and biology, her two least favorite classes. When she had those out of the way, she would be almost glad to study for the others.

When she walked back into Sparrow Hall, she took a left in the lobby and went up the stairs on the guys' side of the dorm, heading for Damon's room on the third floor. He might have plans with the guys, and she sure as hell needed to get some studying done, but that didn't mean she couldn't steal a kiss before he left.

Unfortunately, it was Damon's roommate, Harry

Gershman, who answered the door. Jenna had had maybe three conversations with Harry—an engineering major who always seemed distracted—in the entire first semester. Their conversation at the door was par for the course.

"Hey, Harry. Is Damon around?"

"You just missed him."

"Oh. Okay, thanks."

Harry didn't bother to respond to that. He was shutting the door even before Jenna turned away. She just smiled and shook her head.

As she crossed the common area over to the girls' side of the floor, she heard a phone begin to ring. Realizing that it was coming from her room, Jenna picked up the pace, but by the time she unlocked the door, the answering machine had picked up.

She snatched the phone off the wall. "Hello?"

Dial tone. Whoever called had hung up when the machine came on.

"Humph," Jenna grunted unhappily. "Couldn't have been important."

Annoyed that she had missed the call, she decided to check her e-mail. It was sort of like when her mother promised to make cookies, and didn't get around to it. Jenna always had to have some Oreos or something as a consolation prize.

So, e-mail. Her friends from home, including her closest girlfriends, Moira and Priya, and Noah, a guy both had dated, had been in touch much more in the last week. Christmas vacation was coming, and they'd all see one another again for the first time since college started. Priya had been so strange at Thanksgiving time that Jenna was looking forward to spending time with her, reconnecting.

While she was logging on, the phone rang again.

Jenna was up in an instant and over to the phone. "Hello?"

There was a long sigh. "Jenna." The voice on the other end spoke with a kind of relief, but she didn't recognize it. Not at all.

"Yeah?" she said cautiously. "And this is?"

"I'm . . . I'm back. I'm okay."

Then she knew exactly who it was. *"Dyson?* Geez, Al, where the hell are you? We've been going crazy. Have you talked to Slick? What about Doug? Are you home?"

A pause. Another sigh. "It's . . . it's bad. But I think I know what to do. You've got to meet me . . . at the office. Fifteen minutes."

With a frown, Jenna gripped the phone a bit tighter. "What's wrong, Al? Where are you?"

"Can you meet me?"

"Yeah," she agreed. "I'll be there."

There was a click, and then nothing. Dyson had hung up. Jenna did the same, but then she stared at the phone in consternation for several seconds. Thoughts racing, she went over and shut off her computer, then slipped her leather jacket on over her sweater. She was at the door when her common sense got the better of her. Dyson had been missing. He sounded like hell, and what he'd said made it clear something bad had gone down. It wasn't that she didn't trust him, but she'd been through too much to just walk blindly into a situation that seemed as weird as this one.

Jenna picked up the phone and called Danny at home. The machine picked up, and she left a message, though she had no idea if he'd get it. Just in case, she tried him at the police station, and ended up speaking to another detective, who told her that Danny and Audrey were on duty, but they weren't in the office. With a sigh, Jenna left a message there as well. The detective asked if it was anything important, but the idea of trying to explain something so vague was a bit off-putting, even embarrassing, so she just asked him to have Danny call her.

When she hung up, she looked at the phone one last time, dissatisfied with the results. But there was nothing more she could do. It occurred to her that she might try calling Slick at home, but she wasn't even sure she had the number.

Dyson will have it. We can call from the office.

Her mind whirling with questions and possibilities, Jenna left Sparrow Hall and headed over to Somerset Medical Center. She wanted to be glad that Dyson was all right, and she would be—just as soon as she knew that it was true.

Another bullet bit into the upholstery, and Audrey swore. She risked a quick glance over at Danny. He lay on the beige carpet, blood spreading beneath him, seeping into the carpet in an ever-widening circle. As she watched, his eyes fluttered open, though he still didn't move. But at least there was that. At least he wasn't dead.

For the moment.

She was in a terrible position. If what Dr. Slikowski had said was true, and all the evidence pointed to it, Jason Castillo—the man who had just shot her partner—was still an innocent victim in all of this. That meant she had to do everything in her power not to kill Castillo. Shoot to wound, only. But from behind the chair, there was no way for her to get a good enough look at him to take aim. Any shot would be spur of the moment: jump from cover, and fire. She was sure she could hit him.

But keeping him alive, that was another story.

Not that I'm all that sure I want him alive, she thought angrily. *Son of a bitch is trying to kill me. Never mind the bullet he put in Danny.* But that was just her rage talking. And her fear. For Audrey Gaines was very afraid. Danny had just taken a bullet for the first time in his career. Audrey had never been shot, and she still hoped to avoid it.

That wasn't the worst of it, though. The worst part was the quiet. Castillo was silent. He wasn't shooting his mouth off like every other perp she'd ever run across. Not a word. Apparently, whoever had brainwashed him into this gig hadn't thought to program him with the usual bluster.

"Castillo!" she shouted again. "For God's sake, wake up, you stupid asshole! Wake up!"

The only answer was another bullet. This one tore through the chair, splintering part of the wooden frame as it burst out the back. A tiny shard of wood struck Audrey's face, and she cried out as it cut her. Quickly, she drew a hand up to her cheek, and found blood there.

I'm not dying today, she thought, determined. *Neither is Danny. I hope you don't either, you poor bastard, but if anyone goes down, it's you.*

On the carpet, blood still slowly, inexorably soaking into the carpet, Danny moved, and groaned, tried to speak.

"Danny, stay down!" Audrey shouted. Then she risked the briefest glance around the chair, and her heart froze. Castillo had turned his vacant gaze on Danny, and was about to turn the gun on him as well.

In her mind, Audrey screamed. But her lips remained still, her voice silent. There would be no warning.

With one swift movement, she stepped out from behind the chair, legs spread apart in a shooter's stance, and fired twice. Despite her steady hand and firm stance, the first bullet missed its mark and bit into the plaster wall behind her target. The second took him in the chest, what looked to her to be inches shy of his heart. Castillo's eyes went wide as he staggered back. He looked down at the hole in his chest in disbelief. Though Audrey was stunned that he was still standing, she prepared to fire again. There was no telling how strong the hold on his mind was, if it would keep him going despite the obviously grievous wound.

Then he fell, or, more accurately, crumpled to the floor, dropping to his knees and then toppling over to lie there breathing in ragged gasps. She thought she heard him whisper something in Spanish, and wondered if Jason Castillo finally had his own mind back.

Just in time to die.

"Damn it!" Audrey snarled. *"Nobody's* dying today."

Then she ran for the phone.

Danny could see Audrey. But it was the strangest thing. She was on the phone, and she was talking. That much he could tell. But he couldn't hear anything. It was almost as though he were drowning, ocean water filling his ears. He couldn't really move, either. It was the strangest thing.

And the cold . . . he was so very cold.

The hospital was short-staffed on Sundays. That was always the case. Only emergency surgeries would be performed, and only the E.R. and maternity staffs would be at full strength. When Jenna walked through the lobby at just past ten o'clock, a custodian was mopping in a far corner, but otherwise there was little activity. A stern-looking woman with her hair pulled back in a severe bun sat behind the information desk, and that was all. There was a metal grating pulled down over the front of Au Bon Pain. She presumed it would open after noon, but wasn't certain of that.

Sunday.

Upstairs, on the second floor, the administrative wing was swathed in a weird, almost postapocalyptic silence. Some offices had lights on behind frosted glass, but Jenna knew that was just for appearances. There would be no one inside, for the most part. She heard nothing.

Spooky.

So much so, that she actually spoke aloud to herself, maybe subconsciously hoping to warn away anyone who might be lurking about to frighten her.

"This wasn't your best idea," she assured herself. "You should have waited for Danny."

Or better yet, said no, she thought. For the last time she'd been here during off-hours, with Dyson, they'd found something they had never wanted to find. Now it was Dyson who had asked her here, and she was far more anxious even than logic would dictate.

At the end of the hall, Jenna used her key card to let herself into the medical examiner's office. The click of the lock echoed down the hall. The outer office was empty, but there were lights burning within, just as there had been in some of the other offices she had passed. More than lights, however, there was sound.

Low, pulsing sound. Rhythmic. Melodious.

Within Dr. Slikowski's inner office, beautiful jazz piano lilted softly from the stereo system. Jenna froze, surprised and curious, and a little afraid. *Dave Grusin,* she thought incongruously. *Slick hasn't listened to Grusin in weeks.*

Then, on the heels of that, another thought: *Maybe it's not Slick.*

Reason caught up with her runaway mind quickly enough: If it wasn't Slick, she knew, it could only be Dyson. Probably was Dyson, since he had been the one to call her to come down. Either way, they were her friends. Her employers. She had nothing to fear from them.

Still, she did not call out. She did not saunter into the office and plop herself down in the guest chair, as she might normally have done. Instead, she walked slowly and quietly to the door of that interior office and glanced in.

Behind the desk, Walter Slikowski sat in his wheel-chair, intently studying some paperwork on his desk. Jenna let out a long, quiet sigh of relief.

"Dr. Slik—"

"Dear God, Jenna!" Slick shouted, jumping back in his wheelchair, clapping a hand over his chest. Then he stared at her in horror, breathing heavily. "You nearly did me in. You shouldn't sneak up on a person like that."

"I'm . . . I'm sorry," she stammered. "I didn't mean to, I mean . . ."

"It's all right," he said kindly. Then he smiled and studied her a bit longer. "What brings you down here on a Sunday? One would think between finals and that new boyfriend of yours, you'd have more than enough to keep you busy. Haunted by this case, I'll bet. Just as I've been. Otherwise, I'd be home reading a book or watching old movies right now."

Jenna was a bit taken aback by how chatty Slick was. Not that she didn't understand. He was obviously pleased to see her there. Dyson's disappearance must have been haunting him, and this case wasn't helping, so he had come down to work in peace and quiet, hoping to make some kind of breakthrough. But if she was reading that right—and she was sure she was from his tone and the things he'd said—that meant he didn't know that Dyson was even alive.

"No, no," she corrected. "It's Dyson, actually. He . . . he called me."

Slick was incredulous, but obviously ecstatic. "He's all right? You're kidding. Well, where is he? Never mind that, where *was* he?"

"He didn't tell me," Jenna admitted. "He just asked me to meet him down here. He was all cryptic about it."

"But he's coming here?" Slick asked thoughtfully.

"Yes," Jenna confirmed. "I thought he might already be here."

"Not unless he's invisible."

Before Jenna could reply, the door to the main office clicked open. Jenna craned her neck to see out there, and sure enough, Al Dyson was standing in the open door. As it swung closed behind him, Jenna stared at him with only one thought in her head.

What happened to you?

Dyson looked awful, as though he'd been mugged and then dragged through a dirty alley somewhere. But Jenna was thrilled to see him, nevertheless.

"Al!" she cried, and ran out into the other room, all her fears and anxieties left behind.

Slick came out from behind his desk and propelled his wheelchair into the outer office even as Jenna gave Dyson a tight hug. Immediately, she shrank back from the smell that came off him.

"Are you all right?" she asked, worried for him. "Where've you been?"

For a moment, his eyes were wide and dead, his mouth hanging open as though he might start to drool. Then he blinked and shook his head, and let out a fetid breath.

"I was . . . I don't know, a hostage or something," he

said. "I got away this morning." Dyson looked at Dr. Slikowski then, voice tinged with regret. "I tried calling you first, Walter."

"I've been here, Al," Slick said, voice soft and comforting. "What happened to you? Do you know who it was that did this to you? We've got to call the police immediately."

Dyson looked as though he might throw up. Then he nodded. He was so pale, Jenna wondered if he had been poisoned. If all this was part of the deal with Tim Parish and Shefts and Cohen, she thought it likely he had been.

"We've got to get you to the E.R., too," she said. "And right now." Jenna looked at the M.E. "Dr. Slikowski, if you'll call Danny and Audrey, I'll take him down to the E.R."

Slick nodded. "Get going," he said, and looked at Dyson with growing concern.

Jenna didn't blame him. Dyson seemed completely off, almost shell-shocked. And the way he clutched his stomach, the way he seemed to be in pain, but wouldn't discuss it—he needed help.

"All right, let's go," she said kindly, searching his eyes as she went to him and wrapped one arm around him, letting him put his weight on her to keep from collapsing altogether. Whatever had happened, it was obvious that Dyson had been through something horrible.

"Gotta tell ya, you had us pretty worried. Don't ever run off like that again," Jenna said, trying to bring at least a little levity to the situation.

"I won't," Dyson agreed.

She smiled, about to make another wisecrack as she

helped him toward the door. She was interrupted by Slick's shout.

"Jenna, watch out!"

There was more to it, but she didn't hear the rest. She started to turn, and Dyson moved, far more quickly than she would have thought possible, given how weak he'd seemed even a heartbeat before. His left hand shot out and clutched her throat, cutting off her air, and Jenna began to choke.

In his right hand, he held a long, gleaming hunting knife.

Dyson raised the blade above his head, and brought it down toward Jenna's chest.

chapter 14

Flying. Danny was flying. As he came up into consciousness again, he had an errant thought about angels, but it was gone like the last wisp of a dream as his senses began to kick in, one by one. It began with the copper smell of blood, and the taste of it in his mouth. Then, suddenly, he could hear. There was a kind of orchestral cacophony about him, shouts above his head, a distant electrical voice on a loudspeaker, the *click-clack* of metal on linoleum, people breathing hard, someone speaking to him.

Not flying. For now he could feel the gurney beneath him, every jog and bump, though most of his upper body felt numb and cold. Finally, at the last, his eyes fluttered open, only briefly. There were faces above him, looking down at him, EMTs and nurses, he realized. Lights from the ceiling gave them each an angelic glow.

"Detective Mariano?" someone asked, though he

wasn't sure he'd seen any of them speak. "Can you hear me? Do you know why you're here?"

Danny thought about that for a moment, frowning. *Flying?* He wondered. But no. Not flying. He knew that much. He tried to shake his head, just a bit, to indicate that he did not, in fact, have any idea why he was in the hospital.

"You've been shot," the voice—the nurse?—said, her tone flat. "The doctors are going to take you into surgery now. Just relax, and let them help you."

Danny didn't have the strength to laugh, but he smiled. Or he thought he did; he couldn't quite tell if his facial muscles were responding to his brain's commands. Smiled. *Relax and let them help you,* she'd said. What Danny wanted to say in return was, *I sure as hell don't have anywhere else to go.* But he couldn't manage that.

Instead, he closed his eyes, and let the darkness take him away once more, hoping that he would live to thank these people around him.

Jenna screamed. Her hands came up to defend herself, and she gripped Dyson's arm with all her strength. He tried to force the jagged blade of the hunting knife down toward her face, and she realized instantly that her cause was lost. Al Dyson was a lot stronger than he looked. The blade began to descend, slowly, as he overpowered her.

"No!" she rasped, and tried to swing her leg behind him, tried to knock him over, anything to throw off his balance. It was her only chance.

Dyson drove her forward, using his greater mass to give him leverage, and Jenna slammed into the wall. A framed map of the globe slipped off its nail and the glass broke with a single crack as the frame hit the carpet. Jenna's head bounced off the wall, and she swayed, disoriented.

The blade came down.

Jenna heard Slick shout. "Al, no!"

Then his wheelchair crashed into Dyson. Slick had gotten as much momentum as he could, and when he rammed the chair into his entranced friend, Dyson went over backward, right across Slick's lap. He never lost his grip on the knife, however, not even as Slick grappled with him, trying to wrest the knife away from him. The M.E. wrapped his left arm around Dyson's throat from behind, and began to choke him, but Dyson bucked, and the two men fell out of the chair and onto the floor.

Dyson had the advantage, of course, for unlike Slick, he had the use of his legs. But as Jenna regained her equilibrium and watched them in horror as they struggled on the carpet, she was surprised to see how strong Slick was. He held on to Dyson without any real trouble at all, no matter how Dyson strained to be free. Then she recalled having realized once before that a man who spent every moment of every day propelling himself along by the strength of his arms alone would certainly have developed phenomenal upper body strength.

"Doctor . . . Walter . . ." Jenna said, confused, uncertain what to do. "You're going to kill him!"

"You know . . . better than that," Slick grunted.

He glanced at her, lips drawn back in a grimace as he struggled, and she saw the fear and determination in his eyes, behind the wire-rimmed specs that had miraculously stayed on his face.

Then Dyson rammed an elbow into Slick's gut, knocking the wind out of him, forcing him to loosen his grip. Dyson came up quickly onto his knees above his friend and employer, trying to catch his breath, wheezing even as he brought the knife up.

Jenna ran at them and kicked Dyson, hard, in the back. He stumbled sideways but did not go down. Instead, he came quickly to his feet, and turned on Jenna.

She picked up the broken frame, the only thing near to hand, and flung it at Dyson. He tried to knock it away, but it struck his arm painfully just the same. Dyson glanced at Jenna, and then turned to Slick, who was using his arms to drag himself toward her cubicle.

"Al, please," she said, desperate now.

Jenna rushed him again. Dyson turned to meet her attack with the knife upraised, and she froze. *It's crazy! I can't go after him while he's got that knife!*

"Goddammit!" she roared. "Stop it. You're my friend! What's wrong with you? Even with whatever crap they put into you, you're still my friend under there! Don't you know me, Al? It's Jenna! Please, Al."

But it was useless.

Dyson came at her again.

Terrified, she looked into the dark eyes of this man who was her friend, this man whose tightly curled hair made him look too gentle and even childlike to hurt anyone. But all the kindness and good humor that were usually reflected in his features were gone now.

Jenna knew that in his current state, Dyson would not hesitate to kill her. She raged at him, reached out and slapped him hard across the face. The knife came down, and Jenna ducked, drove her fist into his gut, and tried to spin away from him. With his free hand, Dyson caught her by the back of her sweater. It stretched and she tried to break free, turning to face him again.

Her right hand swung out, fingers curved into claws, and raked her nails across his cheek, drawing blood.

Dyson blinked, seemed thrown off by the pain or the blood or something. Jenna screamed at him, shouted for him to come to his senses. Then she punched him, hard, in the same spot where she'd clawed him. Instead of waking him up further, however, she was horrified to see the opposite reaction. That little glimmer of confusion, of doubt, was suddenly submerged again behind the expressionless, mindless zombie face, the face of the man sent to kill her.

But not just her. *Slick,* she thought, but didn't dare glance around to look for him.

Once again, she was shoved backward. This time she ran into the outer wall of her cubicle. Dyson lunged for her, face dull and slack, and he brought the knife down, the blade glinting in the fluorescent lighting. Jenna brought her left arm up in a block her half brother, Pierce, had taught her, and the blade missed her. With a *thunk,* it stuck in the thick cubicle wall.

As Dyson tried to pull it out, Jenna went to kick him between the legs, but he was expecting it and turned away from the kick, so her foot connected with his calf instead. The knife slipped soundlessly from the hole it had made in the wall. Jenna had space to move at last. She turned to run, but Dyson reached out with his left hand and grabbed her by her hair. Jenna yelped as her scalp blazed with pain.

Her head was back so that her only view was the ceiling. Behind her, in the upper ranges of her peripheral vision, she could see Dyson.

And the knife.

Coming down.

Slick shouted something unintelligible. Dyson seemed to hesitate. Then something hard swung up and struck the arm holding Jenna's hair. Dyson reacted, lurching back, but didn't let go at first, and so Jenna went down on her backside on the floor.

She looked up.

Slick had managed to pull himself back into his wheelchair, with what must have been incredible speed. From somewhere he had retrieved the huge, old-fashioned umbrella he kept in the office for rainy day emergencies. It had a heavy wooden handle, and Slick held it at the top and brought the handle down again. Even as Jenna watched, he struck again with all his considerable strength, this time at Dyson's right arm.

Jenna thought the arm would break, but it didn't. The blow knocked the knife from Dyson's hand, and it went tumbling to the carpet, only inches from Jenna's head.

Dyson's eyes had widened with the blow, and once again, he seemed to hesitate. Then they became dull and vacuous again, and he turned on Slick. Dyson began to rain blows down on his employer, but Slick surprised Jenna once again by proving himself an adept fighter. He blocked most of the blows, and began to land his own to Dyson's abdomen and kidneys, trying to protect himself but also to hurt the other man.

"Jenna!" he snapped as she got to her feet. "Remember Tim Parish? You've got to snap him out of it, or it'll end up him or us. There's only one way to do that!"

Jenna flinched. But she knew immediately that he was right. And she did remember Tim Parish's autopsy, all too well. She thought she'd be dreaming that nightmare for years to come, the kid's eyes opening on the steel table, Tim trying to scream as he looked down to see the slice the scalpel had made in his chest.

The scalpel.

And at her feet now, the serrated hunting knife.

Jenna bent, picked it up, and before she could even question what she knew she had to do, before she could allow her conscience to stop her, she slashed out with the knife and cut a deep gash across Al Dyson's right arm.

Dyson, silent throughout the fight, now screamed.

His eyes cleared as he stared around in shock and horror. He saw Slick's face, bleeding and bruised, then looked at Jenna.

"Oh, my God," he whispered.

Which was when Slick hooked the end of the umbrella around the back of Dyson's leg and pulled, knocking him off his feet.

"Jenna," Slick said, his breath ragged. "Call security. Now."

But she couldn't move. She could only stand there and stare at the knife in her hand, Dyson's blood smeared on the edge. Jenna felt like she might throw up, felt as though she could not catch her breath.

"Jenna!" Slick snapped.

Her gaze turned upon him instantly, but Slick wasn't looking at her. Instead, he was staring intently at Dyson, who lay on the floor, looking disoriented and sad.

Jenna swallowed, and her throat was so dry it hurt. She moved around into her cubicle and dropped the knife on her desk so she could pick up the phone. She had only punched in the first two numbers when the lock on the office door clicked.

Jenna glanced over at Slick, who looked panicked. As far as she knew, very few people had a key card that would let them into this office. The door was pushed roughly open from outside, and Tim Parish entered the room. He held a gun in his hand, and he swept its barrel in an arc across the room as he closed the door behind him. Jenna's mouth dropped open, and she started to shake her head, both unwilling to believe it and angry that she hadn't seriously considered it before.

Tim aimed the gun at her. "Put down that phone," he sneered.

Jenna did as he instructed. As the phone dropped into its cradle, Tim came farther into the room. She could only stare at him, trying to put it together in her head. He'd been out of the hospital a day, maybe two. Nothing made sense.

And everything did.

"You little bastard," Slick sneered.

Though she had been through all of it with him, Jenna was still surprised at the fury in his voice. He seemed nearly all the time to be so reserved, that seeing him so stripped bare of that propriety gave her an entirely new perspective on him, and the kind of emotion he kept bottled up within.

"So now what?" Jenna asked. "You just kill us?"

Tim smiled. It made her feel sick, but when he smiled, Jenna actually felt like smiling with him. He'd seemed so nice before. Not anymore.

"Not exactly," Tim replied. He wore a heavy winter jacket, and now he reached into the pocket and retrieved a small plastic vial. "Gunshots are so very loud. Besides"—the kid grinned, almost embarrassed—"I've still got use for Dr. Dyson, here. And for you, Jenna. The cripple, on the other hand, he'll die."

Jenna bit her lip as it all clicked into place for her. The reason Shefts had done something as stupid as try to rob that bank, the reason Castillo had never been put into action, was because Tim Parish had screwed up and dosed himself with his own poison. She wanted to cry, and not just because of the danger. With great effort, she managed not to look over at Slick.

"Why?" she asked. "All of it. I mean . . . why?"

Tim shrugged and smiled again. Only this time, Jenna wanted to slap that smile off his face.

"It started as an experiment, actually. I did the research, went to the department records at MIT and Harvard. Figured it would be a hoot to try it. I never expected it to work, and when it did, well, it was too good to stop there. I mean, so they smash a place up, steal some valuable stuff, and if they get caught, or anyone gets killed, there's no way in hell to trace it back to me."

"Then Castillo got in the way," Jenna said.

"Yeah. And so did the Somerset cops, and so did all of you."

"Which might never have happened if you hadn't gotten the powder on your skin like a rank amateur," Slick said angrily, moving his wheelchair forward the slightest bit. "You think you're quite clever, but you're really quite stupid. You'd have to be to think you can just go on with this thing. You think you can keep this up forever?"

"Nah," Tim said. "A couple more weeks, that's it. Then I kill all the evidence, or set them up to die, and the experiment's over. No trail, no trace."

"Like hell." Slick moved forward again.

Tim turned the gun on him. "You think you're so smart."

Slick only smiled.

From where he lay bleeding on the ground, Dyson lurched up and grabbed the plastic vial from Tim's hand. Jenna hadn't even noticed that he was back in his right mind, but Slick obviously had. Tim swung the gun over to shoot Dyson, which was when Slick gave the wheels of his chair a massive push, propelling himself at Tim. The kid tried to turn, fired a single shot which went between the two men, and then Slick and Dyson and Tim were all struggling for control of the gun.

"Jenna, run!" Slick shouted.

Dyson started to collapse, his body overcome from its ordeal.

"Like hell," she said, repeating the words Slick himself had said only moments before.

She grabbed the gun with her left hand, and Tim's wrist with her right. With her thumb, she pressed down as hard as she could on the center of his wrist, just below his palm, and his grip slackened—something else Pierce had taught her. Jenna tore the gun from his hand.

Jenna promised herself she wouldn't use it. She couldn't. Stabbing Dyson had been hard enough. There was no way she was going to use a gun. She hated the horrible things.

But Tim kept struggling, kept fighting. He wasn't giving up.

Biting her lip, Jenna raised the gun and pointed it at him.

"Stop," she said uncertainly. Then, more firmly: *"Stop it!"*

There was a gunshot. Jenna flinched, but then realized that it had not come from the gun in her hand. The door to the office was kicked open, and Audrey Gaines stood on the other side, her weapon leveled at Tim Parish.

"On the floor on your belly, you little maggot, or I'll hurt you just on principle."

Tim did just exactly what she said.

e p i l o g u e

On Wednesday, three days after the chaos at the medical examiner's office—which ended, of course, in Tim Parish's arrest—Jenna woke to find herself, for the first time, able to rise without pain. Though her actual injuries had been minimal, she had pulled several muscles, and that had made anything but studying pretty much a painful experience.

She was very well prepared for her Spanish and biology finals.

That morning, as she had the previous two, she took a long shower, letting the hot water steam up the room, the warmth soaking into her muscles. When she got back to her room, she was amazed to find Yoshiko still sleeping. It was very unusual for her to rise before her roommate, but she'd been doing it all week.

Having trouble sleeping. Most of her trouble wasn't with the actual sleeping, but with the dreams that went with it. They would pass, though. She knew they would.

Something else would come up for her to have night-mares about, and the subconscious specter of zombies would be relegated back to *Scooby Doo* reruns on the Cartoon Network.

Jenna pulled on cargo pants and a heavy V-necked Gap top; comfortable clothes were the order of the day. She'd thought about a skirt, and then thought better of it. She decided to forego makeup again in favor of dark sunglasses. The sky outside their two large windows was clear and blue, and though it was fast becoming winter, no one would question the glasses. But they would help.

"Wow," Yoshiko said in a raspy voice, "you almost don't look like a boxer anymore."

Jenna frowned, then winced at the pain the expression caused her. Her face was badly bruised, and though the bruises were healing fast, several of the more significant ones still hurt quite a bit.

"That wasn't funny the first time," she scolded Yoshiko.

"So Hunter tells me. But I guess that's why God gave us all different senses of humor."

Her roommate had such a solemn expression on her face that Jenna couldn't help but smile, and she uttered a short sound that was a combination laugh and grunt of pain. She gave Yoshiko the finger and headed out the door, leather jacket over her arm.

As agreed, Damon was already waiting in the common area. He had wanted to walk with her this morning, and that was just fine with her. Jenna and Damon had spent nearly every waking moment—and some of the sleeping ones—together since the brutal events of Sunday night. He had confessed his fear that she would get sick of him, but so far, she only wanted more. Having him around was everything she'd always believed the whole girlfriend-boyfriend thing should be about. When she had her life to attend to, or he needed to go off and do his thing, each just did. Other than that, they were pretty much together.

"Hey," he said, smiling as he stood up to greet her. Damon tucked the paperback he'd been reading into the pocket of his jacket and reached for her hands. "How's my girl this morning?"

"Getting better," she told him. "Thanks to Doctor Harris."

They kissed tenderly. It hurt her face a little, but she didn't really mind. It was a good kind of hurt. Damon touched her hair as they kissed, and then held her gingerly against him. Then, softly as it had begun, it ended, and they walked hand in hand down the hall to the stairs.

On the walk past the uphill dorms and then across Carpenter Street, their talk was mainly of finals, of Christmas and what they would do with their families over the holidays, and of Jenna's work. But that latter they discussed only a bit.

When they reached Somerset Medical Center, Damon stopped her in the lobby.

"You sure you want to do this?" he asked. "Sometimes it's hard to see someone you care about so . . . vulnerable, y'know?"

Jenna nodded. "I'd like to see him. It'll be okay."

Together, they rode up to the seventh floor and

walked down the corridor to room 712. Jenna paused outside the room. She was about to go in when a tall man in a dark suit came out and nearly ran her over.

"Oh, I'm sorry," he said.

Then he looked at her. "You're Jenna Blake, aren't you?"

For a moment, she didn't recognize him. Then it came to her. "Lieutenant Gonci. I'm sorry. I'm a little scattered this morning."

"I don't blame you," the lieutenant said kindly. "If you've come to see Detective Mariano, however, you might want to try a bit later. He fell asleep a little while ago."

"Oh."

Jenna was disappointed. Damon squeezed her hand, and then she let go and ducked her head into the room. Danny lay on the crisp white sheets with a large IV bottle hanging from a stand by the bed, and two different machines beeping along with the vital functions of his body. He was as white and pasty-looking as any corpse that she'd ever seen on the autopsy table, and his hair had the same stiff, fake quality.

He looked dead.

And if he opened his eyes right at that moment, Jenna thought she might scream.

With a shudder and a sad smile of affection, she drew back from the room. Her first thought was that Damon had been absolutely correct: it disturbed her quite deeply to see Danny so helpless. But in a way, she was relieved that she didn't have to speak to him now, in that state.

"What have you heard from the doctors?" she asked the lieutenant.

"The same," he said grimly. "They've done all they can. They expect a full recovery both for Danny and for Detective Castillo. Danny's mental faculties have apparently not been affected by the loss of blood. But they have to keep an eye on him until he's made a full recovery."

Jenna nodded. "If you see him later, and he's awake, will you tell him I stopped by?"

"I'll do that," Gonci agreed. "And, Jenna?"

"Yes?"

The tall man smiled warmly. "Detective Gaines wrote a very thorough report on the incidents regarding Tim Parish and the medical examiner's office. I just thought I should mention how well that report spoke of you, both for your intuition and your behavior under the pressure of that situation."

Jenna blinked in surprise. "Audrey did that?"

Gonci grinned, and nodded. "Yes," he said. "Audrey did that."

They parted ways. The lieutenant headed back down toward the elevator, but Jenna and Damon lingered behind a few moments. She took another quick glance in at Danny.

"Get better," she whispered.

Damon insisted on riding the elevator down to the second floor and walking to Slick's office with her. Once there, however, he stopped just outside.

"Talk to you later," he said. "Just do me a favor, all right?"

"What's that?" she asked, one eyebrow raised skeptically.

"Stop bringing your work home with you."

"I'll try," she said with a laugh.

The door was open, though that didn't stop Jenna from thinking of the key card in her pocket, identical to the one Tim Parish had taken from Dyson and used to let first Dyson and then himself into the office only days earlier. She shuddered. According to the district attorney's office, it would take months to get Parish's case to court, but the severity of the crimes would be enough to keep him in jail until then, even if it took years to come to trial.

Jenna gave Damon a quick kiss. Then he headed back down the corridor, and she went in. At Dyson's desk there sat a rather sour-looking young doctor, a first-year resident, who had been assigned temporarily by the administration to assist Dr. Slikowski. His name was Nelson, and Jenna didn't like him at all.

"He's been waiting for you," Nelson said dismissively as she entered.

"Thanks!" Jenna said brightly.

She was happy, because according to the doctors, Dyson was supposed to be able to come back to work the following Monday. Her stab wound did more to sideline him than all the poison in his system, but it seemed both problems would be at least substantially cleared up in a few days. Jenna couldn't wait to have Dyson back in the office again. Partially because she missed him, but also because of how skittish he'd seemed the few times they'd spoken since. Al had a complete memory of the things he'd done to her and Slick, and it was haunting him something fierce.

Jenna vowed to work on him, however, and hoped that he'd eventually come around to realizing that he was only a puppet. Not that that was any wonderful thing, either. But it did mean he hadn't actually wanted to attempt to murder his friends.

Her thoughts on Dyson, Jenna walked right past Nelson and into Slick's office. He had Cassandra Wilson's tribute to Miles Davis on the CD player again, and that was a good sign. Once Slick knew that Dyson was going to be all right, his mood had perked up immediately. In truth, she wasn't sure she had ever seen him so energized. It occurred to her to wonder if letting out the pent-up emotions he had kept bottled up so long—in the form of attacking first Dyson and then Tim Parish—had somehow kicked his adrenaline levels into overdrive. Either way, she was pleased at the change in him, no matter how temporary.

"Hey!" she said brightly.

Behind his desk, Slick looked up and smiled. "Glad you're here," he said, adjusting his wire-rimmed glasses. "I've actually been waiting for you. I've got the oddest autopsy to perform today."

"What's that?" Jenna asked, honestly curious.

Slick's smile turned into a devious grin. "Well, it appears that, somehow, toads reproduced inside the subject's chest cavity. Some of them are out, but it seems others died in there. There may even be one or two still alive."

Jenna shot him a harsh, horrified glance. "You're not serious?"

With a small nod, the M.E. moved his wheelchair back from his desk. "I'm completely serious," he said. "I waited for you specifically. I thought if anyone could help me wrap my brain around something as insane as this, it would be you."

Jenna glanced over her shoulder at Nelson, who was glaring at the computer screen in Dyson's cubicle. He was supposed to be assisting Slick now, but the M.E. had told Jenna in private that he didn't feel like breaking someone new in, especially since Dyson was due back soon.

Especially since Jenna could do the job just as well and she knew Slick's work habits. It was only for a few days, he'd told her when they first spoke of it. But he wanted her help.

Toads entombed inside the chest cavity of a human being.

Utter lunacy.

Jenna grinned. "I'm in."

Turn the page for
a preview of
the next
Body of Evidence thriller

HEAD GAMES

Available June 2000

Not long after dawn, two days before Christmas, Jenna Blake stood over the shattered, nearly unrecognizable corpse of the mayor of Somerset, Massachusetts, and struggled to keep from throwing up. The day was gray and cold, threatening snow—Jenna could almost taste it in the air—and the lights from the police cars seemed dull and muted. Powerless. Yellow police tape stretched from a large blue Dumpster to the stone column on one side of the rear stairs of City Hall. Both entrances to the parking lot were blocked by police vehicles to keep civilians away from the crime scene.

But, surreal as it seemed to her, Jenna was there. She'd never met Jim Kerchak, the mayor, before his death. Suddenly, she found herself wondering if he'd been any good at his job; or if maybe he hadn't been, and that truth had led him to take his own life.

Mayor Kerchak's remains had been found just after four o'clock in the morning by a custodian.

"I'll tell ya what ya wanna know," the man had said in his statement to police. "Long as I don't gotta clean it up. Jesus, what a mess."

The custodian was right. It was a horrible mess. Mayor Kerchak's body lay faceup, arms and legs sprawled around him at impossible angles, broken in dozens of places. The splash of blood several feet away indicated that the body had bounced at least once on landing. The back of the mayor's skull had been turned into bone shrapnel, the rest of him just a ravaged pulp of blood and skin, in what had once been a very nice suit.

Jim Kerchak had been a snappy dresser.

The door to the roof of City Hall had been left standing open during the night. Something else the custodian had discovered, this while using the phone to frantically dial 911. It seemed very obvious that Kerchak had done himself in with a swan dive off the roof, but Jenna had been taught almost from day one on the job never to make any judgments about a corpse until an autopsy had been performed.

As she managed to get her gag reflex under control and choke down the burning bile that rose in the back of her throat at the sight of the mayor's brains smeared on the pavement, Jenna turned to look at the man who had taught her that lesson: Dr. Walter Slikowski.

Slick, as she thought of him (but would never call him), was the county medical examiner and widely respected in the field. Local law enforcement often asked him for assistance above and beyond the call of duty. At that moment, she saw, he was deep in thought, brows furrowed with contemplation. Whatever he was thinking about, she could tell by his expression that it wasn't pleasant.

How could it be? His friend is dead.

It had come as a surprise to her that Slick and Kerchak had been friends, but it shouldn't have. Both were men with very little life outside their jobs. By most accounts, Kerchak had been a good mayor. Given her opinion of Slick, Jenna was inclined to believe that.

"What do you think?" she asked quietly.

For a moment, he only sat in his wheelchair and stared at the corpse. She thought he was studying what remained of Mayor Kerchak's face. The man's neck was broken, head at an odd angle. The back of his skull had been destroyed, but the way he struck the ground, the edge of his cheek from temple to jaw had also been pulverized. That part of his face was nothing but pulp; bone and muscle and skin turned to jelly. Jenna thought the white bit she saw jutting from the mess was an edge of shattered jawbone, but she dared not look close enough to confirm that. Her control over the urge to vomit was tenuous, at best.

Dr. Slikowski let out a slow breath and shook his head. He was fortyish and thin, with graying hair and wire-rimmed glasses that gave him a air of hipness that was dispelled as soon as one had a conversation with him. He was a brilliant man, and his mind was always working, which often made him seem distant or distracted when speaking. There was a kind of propriety about him that was almost European, though he had been born and raised in New England.

He still hadn't responded to Jenna's question. She was

about to ask again, to tap his shoulder and try to drag his attention away from the horrid remains of his friend, when Audrey Gaines slipped under the yellow police tape and strode over to them. Jenna glanced around for Audrey's partner, Danny Mariano, but didn't see him. The two were homicide detectives in Somerset, and as such, Jenna and Dr. Slikowski had had ample opportunities to get to know them.

"Hello, Walter," Audrey said, with what passed for compassion from her, but would have seemed cold from anyone else.

"Audrey."

"We can talk later. I just wanted to tell you I'm sorry. I know you and the mayor were friendly."

Slick smiled. "Once upon a time," he said. "Frankly, neither of us had very much chance to socialize of late. But thank you. Have you established what you'll tell the press?"

Audrey took a breath, hesitating. Jenna was surprised. Audrey Gaines rarely hesitated about anything.

"For the moment, we're only confirming that he's dead and that the investigation is ongoing. After the autopsy, we can give them some more."

"All right," Slick said, and nodded. "I'll do it this afternoon."

"Are you sure that's a good idea, Walter?" Audrey asked. "Maybe somebody else ought to take this one."

Slick turned to look at the detective, frowning. "Are you trying to tell me my job, Detective Gaines?"

Audrey blinked, once, then offered a tiny, almost imperceptible shrug. "I'll call you later today, then," she said. Then she turned away from them and went to speak to one of the forensic specialists, a portly man who was in the midst of analyzing the impact point several feet away.

Jenna wanted to say something, to offer some words of comfort, but nothing would come. Audrey was probably right. Psychologically, it was a bad idea for Slick to do an autopsy on a man he'd called friend. Once upon a time, in a horrid nightmare that she frequently wished was only that, and not an actual memory, Jenna had walked in on the autopsy of her own best friend, unaware that Melody was even dead. She had never really gotten over that moment, and doubted that she ever would.

On the other hand, she knew Slick. There was a part of him that simply couldn't allow anyone else to autopsy Jim Kerchak. Mainly because the M.E. didn't trust anyone else to do the job right.

Jenna wanted to say something. More than that, she wanted to go home. The next day was Christmas Eve. Most everyone else on campus was gone already, including her boyfriend, Damon Harris, and her two best friends, Yoshiko—who was Jenna's roommate—and her boyfriend, Hunter. Finals were over and the dorm was abandoned, the campus almost a ghost town.

Jenna had intended to go into work that morning, transcribe the audio records of the two autopsies from the previous day, and go home. It was all set. Her father, Frank Logan, and his fiancée, Shayna Emerson—both of whom were professors at Somerset—were leaving the day after Christmas for a sabbatical in France, and

Frank was lending Jenna his car while they were gone. Freshmen weren't supposed to have cars on campus, but it wasn't really *her* car, and with his faculty sticker, she could park almost anywhere.

She'd had it all worked out.

Then the phone had rung, even before the gray dawn, and Jenna had woken with a start. That early, she knew, a phone call could not be good news. Slick was on the line, with the news of the mayor's death. Now this. Jenna thought she should try to convince him that Kerchak's autopsy should be handled by someone else, for his sake, but also for her own.

She didn't need this, not when the campus felt like the Twilight Zone and all she wanted was to go home. Her things were already packed, except for the antique perfume bottle she'd bought in Harvard Square as a Christmas present for her mother. It was in a box, but she didn't have any wrapping paper, and if she waited much longer to go to the drug store and buy some, Jenna was afraid she'd end up with Daffy Duck birthday paper or something.

Someone shouted behind her, and Jenna glanced quickly around. A cameraman from Channel 7 was trying to get past the cops blocking his path. The blue lights from the police cars painted pale ghosts on the stone wall of City Hall.

"Jenna, what is it?" Slick asked.

She looked at him again, almost surprised to find him watching her. He'd seemed so lost in his own thoughts, in his sorrow. Jenna opened her mouth to tell him she had to go, that this wasn't on her personal holiday agenda. But those weren't the words that came out of her mouth.

"I'll assist you," she told Slick, much to her own astonishment.

The M.E. shook his head. "You should get home to your mother. I'm sure there are plans to be made for Christmas."

Yes. Go home. He told you to go, and you have to wrap Mom's present. Those were her thoughts. But her words . . . her words were different.

"I can go later," she said, mentally cursing herself. "Dyson and Doug are on their way to Aruba by now. I know you don't technically need the help, and I'm no doctor anyway, but I thought, at least, that things went faster when you had someone with you."

Slick couldn't argue with that. "All right. Let's hurry, though. The last thing I want is April Blake blaming me for interfering with her holiday plans."

"She can blame the mayor," Jenna replied.

Slick looked grimly down at the man's corpse. Then he nodded, spun his chair around, and began to propel it back toward his van. Jenna followed, ignoring the cops and the press and the nagging voice in the back of her mind that kept saying *wrapping paper* over and over.

"Tell me what you see."

Jenna was in the middle of using a scalpel to harvest a small sample of Mayor Kerchak's heart tissue. She glanced over at Slick and saw that he was not looking at her, or the heart she was cutting, but at the cadaver on the stainless steel table at the center of the autopsy room. Under the lights, the dead man looked even more horrible than he had before, pale and pasty and grotesque, like some hideous wax museum display.

"What do you mean?" Jenna asked.

Slick nodded at the dead man. "Something's odd here. I was just wondering if you had noticed it."

Jenna managed the tiniest grin. It was a test. When she had first taken the job as pathology assistant at SMC, it was supposed to be mostly clerical work. Over time, however, as Slick had realized that her interest in solving puzzles, and her intuition, were similar in some ways to his own, they had grown into a kind of mentor-student relationship. Jenna's job description hadn't been merely clerical for months.

With another glance at Slick, hoping for some clue from the angle of his gaze, Jenna stepped away from the scale and the partially dissected heart, and began to move around the steel table. It was canted slightly, to allow easier access for Slick in his wheelchair. As she worked her way to the other side, she examined the chest cavity, opened wide by a Y-incision. Nothing out of place there, as far as she could see. Dr. Slikowski had yet to get to the brain, so there was nothing she might have noticed there. The entire front of the body was bruised a deep purple, from toes to genitals to chest. Even part of one cheek, the one not damaged by the impact with the pavement, was flushed almost black. Jenna thought Jim Kerchak might have bounced more than once, given the bruises on him. They . . .

Those aren't bruises.

The realization came suddenly, and her eyes flew open wide as she moved closer to study the body. Jenna paid special attention to the shattered parts of the skull, including the right temple and jaw.

"There wasn't very much blood at the site, was there?" she asked.

"Not very much, no," Slick replied grimly.

Jenna nodded. "I'm with you now."

"Elaborate, if you don't mind," Slick prodded, still testing her.

"I thought it was all bruises from the impact, but the dark 'bruising' is the effect of the settling of the blood after death," she said.

Slick smiled softly and nodded for her to continue.

"The body sat for hours before being discovered. He was faceup, and only the rear of his body badly damaged by the impact. Which means that the only way for this kind of settling to have occurred is if he was killed hours earlier—long enough for the blood to begin to settle—and then thrown off the roof."

"I think we'll find that his neck was broken," Slick explained. "Of course, only finishing the autopsy will allow us to confirm that."

The medical examiner smiled. "Well done, Jenna. I'm proud of you. Now let me finish up down here. You get on home."

Uncomfortably, Jenna shifted her weight. "Are you sure?"

"Very. I'll take it from here. Go home and enjoy your Christmas. You've earned it."

"Okay," she agreed, stripping off her bloody gloves and slipping out of her white lab coat. "But while Dyson's away, if you really need my help, just call and I'll come right out, okay? I have my dad's car, so it's no problem."

"I'll do that. You go on. Drive safely, and Merry Christmas."

Jenna dropped her lab coat on a pile of laundry. As she pushed out the door, she called back to him. "Merry Christmas to you, too, Dr. Slikowski."

But Slick barely acknowledged her. His attention was back on the corpse of his friend, the mayor, whom it now seemed had been murdered. Any trace of a smile had been erased from Slick's face.

In that moment, it seemed impossible to Jenna that Christmas was only two days away.

Look for the next
Body of Evidence **thriller**
HEAD GAMES
by Christopher Golden

about the author

CHRISTOPHER GOLDEN is the award-winning, *L.A. Times*–bestselling author of such novels as *Strangewood* and the three-volume *Shadow Saga; Hellboy: The Lost Army;* and the *Body of Evidence* series of teen thrillers (including *Thief of Hearts* and *Soul Survivor*), which is currently being developed for television.

He has also written or cowritten a great many books, both novels and nonfiction, based on the popular TV series *Buffy the Vampire Slayer.*

Golden's comic-book work includes the recent *Wolverine/Punisher: Revelation* and stints on *The Crow* and *Spider-Man Unlimited*. Upcoming projects include a run on *Buffy the Vampire Slayer; Batman: Real Worlds* for DC; and the ongoing monthly *Angel* series, tying into the *Buffy* television spin-off.

The editor of the Bram Stoker Award-winning book of criticism, *CUT!: Horror Writers on Horror Film,* he has written articles for the *Boston Herald, Disney Adventures,* and *Billboard,* among others, and was a regular columnist for the worldwide service BPI Entertainment News Wire.

Before becoming a full-time writer, he was licensing manager for *Billboard* magazine in New York, where he worked on Fox Television's *Billboard Music Awards* and *American Top 40* radio, among many other projects.

Golden was born and raised in Massachusetts, where he still lives with his family. He graduated from Tufts University. He is currently at work on his next novel, *Straight on 'Til Morning*. Please visit him at www.christophergolden.com.

. . . A GIRL BORN
WITHOUT THE FEAR GENE

FEARLESS™

A NEW SERIES BY
FRANCINE PASCAL

A TITLE AVAILABLE EVERY MONTH

Prue, Piper, and Phoebe Halliwell
didn't think the magical incantation
would really work. But it did.
Now Prue can move things with her
mind, Piper can freeze time, and
Phoebe can see the future. They are
the most powerful of witches—
the Charmed Ones.

2387

Everyone's got his demons....

ANGEL™

If it takes an eternity, he will make amends.

❖

Original stories based on the
TV show created by Joss Whedon
& David Greenwalt

2311

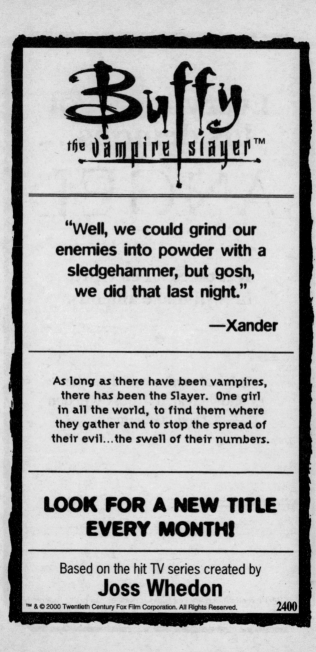

Buffy
the Vampire Slayer™

"Well, we could grind our enemies into powder with a sledgehammer, but gosh, we did that last night."

—Xander

As long as there have been vampires, there has been the Slayer. One girl in all the world, to find them where they gather and to stop the spread of their evil...the swell of their numbers.

LOOK FOR A NEW TITLE EVERY MONTH!

Based on the hit TV series created by
Joss Whedon

2400